Titles by *Langaa* RPCIG

Francis B. Nyamnjoh
Stories from Abakwa
Mind Searching
The Disillusioned African
The Convert
Souls Forgotten
Married But Available

Dibussi Tande
No Turning Back. Poems of ⋯

Kangsen ⋯
Fragments ⋯

Ntemfac ⋯
Namondo. Child of ⋯
Hot Water for the ⋯

Emmanuel Fru ⋯
Not Yet Damas⋯
The Fire Within
Africa's Political Wastelands: The Bastardization of Cameroon
Orik'badan

Thomas Jing
Tale of an African Woman

Peter Wuteh Vakunta
Grassfields Stories from Cameroon
Green Rape: Poetry for the Environment
Majunga Tok: Poems in Pidgin English
Cry, My Beloved Africa
No Love Lost

Ba'bila Mutia
Gods of Mortal Flesh

Kehbuma Langmia
Titabet and the Takumbeng

Victor Elame Musinga
The Barn
The Tragedy of Mr. No Balance

Ngessimo Mathe Mutaka
Building Capacity: Using TEFL and African Languages as Development-oriented Literacy Tools

Milton Krieger
Cameroon's Social Democratic Front: Its History and Prospects as an Opposition Political Party, 1990-2011

Sammy Oke Akombi
The Raped Amulet
The Woman Who Ate Python
Beware the Drives: Book of Verse
Susan Nkwentie Nde
Precipice

Francis B. Nyamnjoh &
Richard Fonteh Akum
The Cameroon GCE Crisis: A Test of Anglophone Solidarity

Joyce Ashuntantang & Dibussi Tande
Their Champagne Party Will End! Poems in Honor of Bate Besong
Emmanuel Achu
Disturbing the Peace

Rosemary Ekosso
The House of Falling Women

Peterkins Manyong
God the Politician

George Ngwane

The Power in the Writer: Collected Essays on Culture, Democracy & Development in Africa

John Percival
The ⋯ Cameroon Plebiscite: Choice or Betrayal

Albert Azeyeh
⋯aillite sociale : généalogie mentale de la ⋯"Afrique noire francophone

⋯b Amin & Jean-Luc Dubois
⋯éveloppement au Cameroun : ⋯brée à un développement équitable

⋯son Anyangwe
⋯alistic Politics in Cameroun: ⋯srance & the Inception of the Restoration of the Statehood of Southern Cameroons

Bill F. Ndi
K'Cracy, Trees in the Storm and Other Poems

Kathryn Toure, Therese Mungah
Shalo Tchombe & Thierry Karsenti
ICT and Changing Mindsets in Education

Charles Alobwed'Epie
The Day God Blinked

G.D. Nyamndi
Babi Yar Symphony
Whether losing, Whether winning

Samuel Ebelle Kingue
Si Dieu était tout un chacun de nous?

Ignasio Malizani Jimu
Urban Appropriation and Transformation : bicycle, taxi and handcart operators in Mzuzu, Malawi

Justice Nyo' Wakai:
Under the Broken Scale of Justice: The Law and My Times
John Eyong Mengot
A Part of Ages

Ignasio Malizani Jimu
Urban Appropriation and Transformation: Bicycle Taxi and Handcart Operators

Joyce B. Ashuntantang
Landscaping and Coloniality: The Dissemination of Cameroon Anglophone Literature

Jude Fokwang
Mediating Legitimacy: Chieftaincy and Democratisation in Two African Chiefdoms

Michael A. Yanou
Dispossession and Access to Land in South Africa: an African Perspevctive

Tikum Mbah Azonga
Cup Man and Other Stories

Cup Man and Other Stories

Tikum Mbah Azonga

Langaa Research & Publishing CIG
Mankon, Bamenda

Publisher:
Langaa RPCIG
(*Langaa* Research & Publishing Common Initiative Group)
P.O. Box 902 Mankon
Bamenda
North West Province
Cameroon
Langaagrp@gmail.com
www.langaapublisher.com

Distributed outside N. America by African Books Collective
orders@africanbookscollective.com
www.africanbookscollective.com

Distributed in N. America by Michigan State University Press
msupress@msu.edu
www.msupress.msu.edu

ISBN:9956-558-41-9

© Tikum Mbah Azonga 2009
First published 2009

DISCLAIMER

Contents

1

Cup Man

Pa Shimoon, for that was what we grew up knowing him to be called, was an extraordinary man. When I First heard of the name of the former Israeli Prime Minister, Shimoon Peres - and that was in primary school - it reminded me of Pa Shimoon's name. I sometimes wondered if the name Shimoon was not really a corruption of Simon, but my father said it was not.

"His father named him Shimoon. I don't know why, but that's the name his father gave him at birth. If you want the whole story, his full names are Shimoon Atanga Ngu, the last name being his father's," my father would say, and then go on to recall that Pa Shimoon's father ran into problems with the parish priest who stopped the local priest from baptizing Pa Shimoon, unless he was given a "proper" Christian name, whatever he meant by "proper".

"We can't put that name on our church records. It's not a Christian name. It must be a pagan creation," Fr. Anthony said, in the coolness typical of Mill Hill missionaries. He was born in Southampton but grew up in Bedfordshire and Yorkshire. However, since Pa Shimoon's father would not agree to an alternative name and the parish priest would not yield an inch either, a rift soon developed between the two men. The result was that Pa Shimoon's father withdrew his entire family from the Catholic Church and they became Presbyterians. Of course, my father could afford to be so authoritative about Pa Shimoon. Both men were from Njini Menam village. They were age mates and had grown up together in the village. They were classmates in the village catholic Mission Primary School. When Pa Shimoon's father moved them out of the Catholic Church, he accordingly enrolled at the village Presbyterian school. Meanwhile my father stayed on at the St. Andrew Catholic School. When

1

both boys completed primary school they entered the big and famous Basel Mission College (B M C) that was the only one for boys in that part of the country. After their studies, they both won British scholarships to study in England. My father went to the famous Milroe College where he took an honours degree in Tropical Agriculture. His friend and brother went to Silverpool for and honours in mechanical engineering. That was then. Today, because of the closeness of my father and Pa Shimoon, all of us my father's eight children (from his only wife, my mother, mama Benedicta) called Pa Shimoon, just Shimoon, not uncle Shimoon. The latter, on the other hand, had two wives. Mama Beatrice had five children while the second wife, Mama Angela, had three. If you ask me, I would say Pa Shimoon had difficulties handling his polygamous home because there were frequent fights between the wives. Sometimes they even they fought.

Even so, what I or I guess any other child with whom I grew up in the neighbourhood remember most about Pa Shimoon was his indulgence in alcohol. It seemed to me that he was always drunk.

For many years he and my father worked in Ndokoban, the headquarters of Kana administrative Division in the Plateau Province. My father was the divisional delegate for Agriculture while Pa Shimoon was Divisional Chief of service for Agricultural Statistics. My father was his boss because according to the organisational chart, the Divisional Delegate of Agriculture Controlled the Divisional Chief of services for Administration and Finance, the Divisional Chief of Community Development, the Divisional Chief of Rural Engineering, the Divisional Chief of Agriculture Production.

My father always spoke disconsolately about his "brother Shimoon" at home. "What haven't I said to him? I have warned him repeatedly about drinking. I have told him it will ruin his career and even his life. But will my brother listen to me? That places me in an awkward situation because if I were to apply the rules on him and send a nasty report to hierarchy, he might lose his job. But does my brother understand that?"

Sometimes, I felt sorry for Pa Shimoon because even his physical looks were already wearing him down. He, from what I could see was born handsome. He had the fair complexion, which most people dream of. Unfortunately he made himself a slave to alcohol. Perhaps he could even have been a delegate like my father. Let's not talk about smoking because they both smoked, and in all fairness to Pa Shimoon, they smoked sparingly. Pa Shimoon's greatest sin was alcohol abuse and drunkenness, not smoking.

One morning when my father sent me to Pa Shimoon's place to get something for him I found Pa Shimoon lying in bed, drinking whisky straight from the bottle as if it was water. The room stank of alcohol.

Surprisingly, his first wife, Mama Beatrice, as she prepared her husband for work, and the children for school, repeatedly entered the room but showed no sign of surprise or disgust. I suppose the poor woman was, after these many years of marriage to an ever drunk husband, simply braved things out. Otherwise, what could she do about it? Pa Shimoon would not listen. However, perhaps the poor man too was now too addicted to alcohol to come out of the situation. So after I stepped into his bedroom and found him drinking his whisky, I stood respectfully, waiting for him to finish. "Good morning Pa," I said.

"Good morning, my child," he replied turning round with difficulty and groaning about pains all over his body. But he made sure he held very tightly to his half drunk bottle of whisky. He looked worn out, tired and sleepy. Surely, he must have been drinking in one of the off license or bars in the town the previous night. "In such a state, how will he go to the office today?" I wondered to myself. Of course, I would never dream of putting such a question to him. I knew he would beat me, and report me to my father who would again beat me without giving me the slightest chance in the world to defend myself.

3

Pa Shimoon finally managed to sit up in bed, and I had no choice than to put up with that very strong and offensive smell of alcohol.

"Is it…Is it… Arrr… rrr! You …Captain?"

"Yes Pa." I replied. He always addressed me as "captain," because as he said, he was sure I would grow up to join the national armed forces and eventually become a captain. Time was to prove him right because after my degree in law, I passed the entrance examination into the National Military School and later became a captain. Using my law degree, I trained at the national administration and magistracy school and became a military magistrate. I retired a couple of years ago as a colonel. So on that one, Pa Shimoon got things right.

Back in his smelling room he asked why I had come. "Pa asked me to get the leave requisition file from you."

"Oh yeah? Is that all? Your father didn't send me anything?"

"No, Pa."

"Why not? He didn't send me any whisky? Or even a beer, for my breakfast?"

Here, there was no way I could hold back: "Alcohol for breakfast, Pa?"

"Yes, of course, captain. Why not? By the way, what class are you in?"

"Class seven, Pa."

"So you are due secondary school this year? And you don't know that alcohol is good for breakfast? What do your teachers teach you these days? I don't…"

Here, he raised his bottle and gulped down a mouthful rather absent-mindedly.

"Yes, this makes me feel good!" he said, making grimaces because of the drink. I noticed he was still in his pyjamas and had not had a bath. If he was as time-conscious as my father, he should be in the office in exactly an hour. The time by his old clock was 7 o'clock. But knowing him well, I was sure he would get to the office after his boss.

He had struggled to his feet, still clutching his bottle.

4

"That bloody file! Where is it? Where did I put it?"

For once, he put his bottle on the table, fetched his black brief case, and placed it on the table and after about five minutes of figuring out how to open it, the brief case flung open. He ransacked it. All this while I ran towards him several times because he was staggering and I felt he might fall.

"No! No! No! captain… I'll be all right. Do you now see why your father should have sent me a bottle?" he mumbled.

"Yes, Pa" I acquired, most reluctantly, for although I was only a little boy, I never liked sacrificing my principles. I felt I was betraying myself. How on earth could Pa Shimoon prescribe alcohol for breakfast? I had never heard or read about that anywhere and to be frank with you, I did not believe there was any teacher who could make such a claim.

After searching in vain for the file, he mumbled something to the effect that I should tell my father he would give him the document in the office. Before I left, Pa Shimoon had crashed back in bed, his bottle beside him. He started snoring like and old cow.

When I got home and gave my father the message, his reaction, which was, of course, addressed to himself, was: "I knew it. How could he find it?"

From what we occasionally overheard our father telling our mothers at home, Pa Shimoon was equally a disaster at work. He knew his job well. Remember he was a mechanical engineer, appointed to the post of agricultural statistics chief. So, from any perspective, he was a square peg in a square hole. In fact, not only had he always been good at mathematics, but also at the Advanced level, he scored distinctions in mathematics with statistics, applied mathematics, statistics (as a whole subject), Physics and Chemistry. So, when he applied himself to his job, he did it well. The problem unfortunately was that since he was often drunk, his job was often poorly done.

At such times, he would arrive for work late and no sooner had he settled down than he would disappear from the office, leaving his door open, consciously or unconsciously. People waiting to see him would grow impatient and leave with their files untreated. Once his boss, my father, sent for him. When the messenger returned to my father and reported that the door was open but the chief was absent, my father ordered the Chief of Service for Administration and Finance to lock the door, get some men and comb all the drinking places in the town and bring him to the office. Pa Shimoon was found in an off license, drinking with the left hand and sighing documents of waiting service users with the right hand. While doing so, he talked about things that had no bearing on the work he was doing. He was completely off topic. When the men reported back to the Divisional Delegate, he thanked them and asked them to leave him alone with Pa Shimoon. Turning to Pa Shimoon, he said, "Sit down, please."

My father was making a big effort to control himself and sound courteous. Even so, Pa Shimoon spoilt it all because in the process of sitting, as he was staggering, he missed the seat by sitting too far away from it. As he struggled to regain his balance, he grabbed my father's table and accidentally scattered some of the effects on it on the floor.

"What nonsense is this? I pull you out of an off license during working hours, and as if that is not enough, you scatter my table? Look at how you tremble like a leaf and fall like a child! What is all this slavery to alcohol, Shimoon?"

"Sorry… I'm sorry, boss … I …"

"Well, that will help neither you nor me. My God how you stink of alcohol!"

Then my father continued in our mother tongue, Ngam Njini Menam (literally, the language of Njini Menam).

"Shimoon, you are a disgrace to me. The whole of this town knows you and talks about you very negatively. Alcohol will ruin you! Are you happy to have earned yourself a notorious nickname like, Cup Man?"

"I … I …"

At that point he had still not managed to get up from where he had fallen. So my father went round the table, gave him a hand and helped him up.

"Look at how you have soiled your clothes! How will you walk in the streets?"

My father sent for his driver and asked him to take Pa Shimoon home. Before he left, my father told him: "Shimoon, I've just been told Beatrice and Angela have quarrelled at home and are fighting. Go and see what you can do."

"My wives?"

"Yes your wives."

Pa Shimoon was helped into the vehicle, a Toyota Four Wheel Drive. As they drove past, occasionally, people would point at him and say, "Look! There goes Cup Man!"

One day, the Senior Divisional Officer paid a surprise visit to the Divisional Delegation of Agriculture. When the Delegate did roll call, everyone was present apart from Yours Faithfully.

"Where is Shimoon?" he asked the Chief of General Affairs and Finance.

"I haven't seen him all morning, Delegate."

"Okay, check first at his home, then in the drinking places. Bring him discreetly when you find him. I'll make sure the Senior Divisional Officer visits all the other services first to give him enough time to get back. Let's hope he is sick or just tired, not drunk. For God's sake, not drunk again!"

He was found in an off license, drunk and insulting the people drinking with him. He created a scene because first, he refused to pay for the six large bottles of Castle he had drunk, on the grounds that he had drunk only three and was being "fraudulently" made to pay for six. His colleagues asked him to pay for the three he recognized. Then they contributed money and paid for the other three. However, there was still trouble because he now insisted he must leave with the unfinished bottle. In vain his colleagues explained that the Divisional Officer was visiting. In vain the bar saleswoman tried to explain to him that if he must go with the bottle he must first pay a refundable deposit on it. His refusal was categorical.

"You are an old, dirty and stinking prostitute!" he told the woman.

"Look here, Cup Man. If I didn't know exactly who you were, I would be annoyed. Now that I know you, I can only feel sorry for your wives and children."

Thereupon, Pa Shimoon flew into a rage. "My family! How dare you insult my family? Leave me alone. Let me… Let me teach this swine a… lesson!"

His companions now decided the only option was force. So, they grabbed the bottle from him, returned it to the woman, and bundled him away kicking and cursing. He was forced into the vehicle. The men decided that since the situation was much worse than they had anticipated, they must find some way of advising the Delegate not to reveal him to the Senior Divisional Officer in that state.

Unfortunately, just as they were getting him out of the vehicle, the Senior Divisional Officer emerged from the building accompanied by the Divisional Delegate and the Senior Divisional Officer's entourage. The Administrator stopped abruptly on seeing and hearing Pa Shimoon who was speaking hysterically and insolently about the bar woman. The words the Senior Divisional Officer heard distinctly were: "That prostitute! She took my unfinished bottle of beer! I will teach her a lesson!"

"Who is that man, Delegate? You know I haven't been long in this Division to know all your collaborators. Is he one of them?"

Yes, Monsieur le Préfet. That is Mr. Shimoon Atanga Ngu. He is our Divisional Chief of Service for Agricultural Statistics."

"Is he always like this, Delegate?"

"No, Monsieur le Préfet. Not always. Sometimes. Not always."

The Senior Divisional Officer went nearer.

What trouble are you having gentleman?"

"Trouble? You ask me about trouble? Where is my beer? You..."

"Mr. Ngu, don't talk like that to the Prefect!" barked my father.

"Prefect? What Prefect? I have no Community Development with any Prefect. I keep statistics, agricultural statistics. I..."

Mr. Ngu!" snapped my father.

"That's okay, Delegate. Within the hour I will have to issue you a query. That will be for inability to control your staff. My visit is over. Thank you for the reception."

And he left at once. By this time, Pa Shimoon had been left alone. He was staggering towards his office. When he got there and found it had been locked, he could not find his keys. So, he started kicking the door saying very incongruous things such as, "I know you are in there stealing my food, Platoon Soldier. Come out, you starving nincompoop!"

Platoon Soldier was his dog at home. He was also saying, "Hey you bar woman! What are you doing with my drink? Do you want to urinate in it before you give me? You fool! Has a woman ever urinated in a bottle? Ha! Ha! Ha!"

Thereupon he slumped against the door and went down like a sack of corn. Almost immediately, he started snoring. When the Divisional Delegate was informed, he came to see for himself.

"God Almighty! Have I not had enough of my share of troubles for the day?"

He instructed his driver and two other men to take Pa Shimoon home. The time was 11.10, fifteen minutes after the Senior Divisional Officer stormed off. At exactly 11.50, a messenger from the Senior Divisional Officer brought the query my father had been threatened with by the Senior Divisional Officer. Within an hour, my father too had addressed his own query to Pa Shimoon. His intention was to attach Pa Shimoon's reply to his before taking it to the Senior Divisional Officer. That was what he did.

In the end, although the Prefect understood that the fault was really that of Pa Shimoon and gave him a poor end of year mark, the fact remained that Pa Shimoon had not gone down alone. He had brought my father down with him because the query to my father and its reply was still placed in my father's file. In other words, my father's file had a stain.

Pa Shimoon's disgrace with alcohol did not end there. Many were the times he got home very late at night, sometimes after falling and rolling in mud several times. There were times when he had to be taken home by "Good Samaritans" who found him asleep on a chair in an off licence after everyone else had left and the barmaid was cursing. Worse happened for he was once found sleeping in a gutter one early morning after failing to return home. He smelt of urine and excreta.

Hearing this, one may wonder whether no medical person ever warned him about the dangers of alcohol to his health. Of course, they did! Doctors and even nurses, but he wouldn't listen.

Once his situation became so serious that the doctors after examining him said he had early signs of cancer of the throat. He was admitted in hospital. After a week, his condition started improving. Then Pa Shimoon, who had all along been moaning about being "killed slowly by being deprived of drink" which he called his food, came up with a plan. He bribed someone to buy whisky and sometimes beer, and put it in a tea flask and deliver it to him in hospital as if it was tea. When he was a lone and found that no one was noticing, he would quickly have a drink, close the flask and stand it back on his bedside hospital cupboard. One day, nurse Naomi surprised him with a flask in bed. When asked, he said he was feeling cold and needed to warm himself up with the flask. It's just that at that juncture the usually alert nurse was distracted by another patient, otherwise the thought would have crossed her mind that the outer part of a flask is not warm since all the heat is inside. Although the doctor, nurses and ward servants sometimes smelled alcohol in Pa Shimoon's space, they never accused him, for want of evidence. So, the patient continued "cheating". His situation got worse until it got to a point where he was weak. Still, he managed to get his innocent six-year old son who happened to be with him, to open the flask and give him. For some strange reason, perhaps because his time had come, he drank too much whisky and died in his sleep. The uncorked whisky got spilled all over the bed, beneath the blanket and stank from afar. When Nurse Naomi found him in that state, she exclaimed:

"Oh My God! So this is what it was all about?"

In less than no time, the entire town had known that Cup Man was no more. He died the way he lived. By the cup.

2

The mad Cow

Balemba village was blessed in the sense that it had only high school in the province. By high school I mean an institution where students were prepared for the G.C.E. advanced Levels. Because the high school was the lone one, students who obtained the G.C.E. Ordinary Level from the many secondary schools in the province vied for places at the Bangara college of Education, as it was known. It was called a college because the government intended to upgrade it to an institution that could then award HNDs. But that has never really happened. You know how it is with bureaucracy. Anyway, that is another story.

Bangara College was an entirely boarding school whose students were adults (aged over 18) and treated as such. For instance, they were served fish three days a week, chicken two days and meat two days. They ate well with their meals being varied and rich. Each of the three items had a supplier. For example, chicken was supplied on Tuesdays Thursdays and Saturdays, chicken on Wednesdays and Saturdays. Meat, and that is what our story is about, was provided on Fridays and Sundays. The incident I am about to recount happened on a Friday and concerns a cow that went mad. But first, a description of the topography of the area will help the reader to understand the incident better.

To go to the college, one had to branch off the trunk road that cut through the urban district of the village. Taking the right hand branch that was opposite the one leading to the college would mean go to the hinterlands of the village and eventually the Fon's Palace, which was three miles away. However, a mile before the palace was a left branch leading to the cattle market. It was the largest cattle market in the group of five villages in the area. Trading took place there every Friday and on such a day, around fifty cows were sold there. Two men, one of whom from the front, pulled and directed the animal from a leash tied to its neck, took them away. Another from the back held a leash tied to the beast's leg. He would pull if the cow were moving too fast and therefore posing a threat to the foreman.

****

On the Friday morning of the incident, early morning buyers were coming away from the cattle market with their cows being herded by the foreman and the hind man.

"Gafara!" the hind man would say, lashing out at the cow with his whip, if the animals slowed down unnecessarily or started changing direction into the bush.

"Hai! Hai!" said the foreman to warn pedestrians that a cow was coming down. The warning was necessary because sometimes some cows became very wild and would charge at onlookers, thus throwing them in disarray and even causing some of them to lose balance in the stampede, fall down and injure themselves or be trampled upon.

Despite the danger, little children loved taunting cows by rubbing their neck with their hand thus telling them that they were going to be killed. To stress the point, the boys would stamp their right feet on the ground. One would normally think that a cow, being only an animal, would not understand that kind of language, let alone its implication. But far from it, they did. That is why any cow thus teased, would take offence and thus charge at the provoker. At such a position both fore man and hind man would summon all their might to control the enraged beast. Often they hurled abuses at the poor animal murmuring in Fulani, the language of the majority cattle grazers in the region, or in their own language or in pidgin.

"You cow! No start da your nonsense!"

Meanwhile, the little school boys, feeling they had their joke, after all, would laugh while running away at a speed neither the cow nor the two herdsmen could match.

On the day of the incident, one cow that was being led out of the cattle market started the day on a bad note. After the herdsmen had tied a nozzle and successfully flung it around the neck of the cow, they secured it, and then skilfully provoked the cow into putting its right foot into another nozzle that had been purposely placed on the ground. Quick as a flash, the hind man leapt at it and pulled it so that it got tightly secured on the cow's leg. For this unfortunate cow, of all the cows that left the cattle market on that day, none went through as many tribulations as Ali, for that was the name the cow was given by the original owner who raised it.

As there was a school, a Catholic primary school so close to the cattle market, it turned out that once the two herdsmen and Ali stepped onto the motor road just outside the market, they ran into a group of deviant children who started booing the cow and hurling stones at it. As might be expected, some of them made the death sign to Ali. It took a lot of shouting and threats of beatings from the two herdsmen for the boys, six in number, to disperse.

For Ali though, it was too late. He had been worked up beyond the point of no return. The foreman and his counterpart noticed this at once, for Ali's countenance had changed. He was headstrong and stamped his feet, instead of galloping. The two herdsmen had been in the business long enough, that is thirteen years, to know when an animal was turning into a beast.

So, not even the friendly taps on the back of the animal or the fondling of his male genitals meant anything to this offended mammal. As a result, the warning calls from the foreman to onlooker and passersby were more strident. Some understood the danger and immediately took cover. But again, the children walking to school continued to be a stumbling block, as they continued to taunt the cow. At one point, the hind man almost lost control of his leash as the animal suddenly made a dash for some boys who provoked it and were trying to escape. But the foreman was an old hand. Within a few minutes, he had brought back Ali under control.

By the way, it is not haphazardly that the foreman and the hind man are chosen. The foreman is usually hefty and strong so that single-handedly he can pull the cow back if necessary. The foreman is by any standard an athlete who can run faster than the cow, if it were to break free from the hind man. That was exactly what the two men on this day were. Even so, this was not to be their day for their cow received more provocation on the way than any other cow they had ever led away from the market. These constant interruptions made the journey unnecessarily long.

****

Back at the college where the cooks were expecting the cow, there was beginning to be some agitation as already the cow was an hour late. Usually it got there by nine, after which the two herdsmen were paid extra to slaughter it and cut it up into major parts such as the head, the two thighs, the two forequarters, the neck, the inside contents, the four legs, and the skin. The rest was left to the cooks, under the supervision of the Chief cook.

Usually the Principle allowed the cooks and stewards to share among themselves the head, the tail, the intestines and the four legs. The legs were no problem because, since they were four and the kitchen staff four, sharing was easy. For other parts like the tail and the intestines, they shared them simply. When it came to the head, they agreed that it was never a good thing to share a head because it would be like casting lots over a head made by the Almighty God. That in turn could bring them ill luck. So they decided that member would have a turn in carrying the whole head home. On this day the notorious cow was expected, it was the turn of the Chief cook, Godlove, as students were fond of calling him. That was his name, anyway. The point is that the same stude4nts called the other kitchen staff by their surname, in some cases prefixing it with "Mr." But perhaps the problem with Godlove was that of familiarity breeding contempt. Of all the kitchen staff, he was the only one who at night, would throw off his work clothes, have a good bath, put on his "show boy" clothes, perfume himself and go dancing in the one and only night club in the vicinity, called Spot Bar. Here he rubbed shoulders with students from Bangara College. They sat together, danced together, and drank together and cracked jokes together. He got a chance to dance with the prettiest girls. He could even dance blues that enabled him to press girls' breasts to his chest and feel good or "high as he used to put it. When it came to dancing rock, which most people found difficult, Godlove was always a champion. Everyone who went to nightclub knew him. He was a star in his own way. In fact, once in a while, in the night club a certain Dominic, would buy him a free drink, because let's face it, he also attracted customers to the bar in terms of the number of people who came there just to see Godlove.

Back on the road, the going was getting tougher and tougher. Children's taunts had worked up the cow so much that it was annoyed just with anyone and saw everyone as a threat, even the two herdsmen who knew it by name.

Of the three kilometres journey, the cow had made only two kilometres, which was slow. They were now by passing the late Pa Nebashi's compound down below on the left. The late man made his name in the village by being the first man from there whose son became a headmaster, and the only one whose son became the first headmaster of the village school, St. Joshua's School. On this day, the herdsmen and the cow had left the market at the usually 7:30am. Normally, by the time it was, that is, 9:30am, they should not still be at Pa Nebashi's compound, a compound which they always get to at about 8:45am. So, today must be really a bad day. Amungwa the senior herdsman said to himself.

"Ashanga, this is not a good journey we are having today," he said to his companion.

"It is certainly not," Fundum replied, "As they talked over the cow to each other, it groaned loudly as if to say they were disturbing him.

16

"Oh, shut up, you cow! You've given us enough trouble for one day already!" Ashanga shouted.

The cow was panting heavily as it galloped also Saliva was trickling down its mouth, often a sign that he was exhausted or thirsty, or both. But the foreman and hind man in no mood to compromise and let it have a drink of water.

"When they got to the bridge over the street that was between the area where Pa Nebashi's compound was and "God's Promise" off licence, the animal came to an abrupt stop and refuse to continue, regardless of what was done or said to it. The senior herdsman called it all kinds of names in all kinds of tones.

"Debo!" (Woman in Fulani)

"Ndjala ku!" (Nonsense)

"Bi wa ad dere djo!" (You good for nothing)

The reason why the herdsman chose to address the cow in Fulani was because the bulk of cattle rearers in the country were Fulani. So everyone had the general belief that cattle were first and foremost a Fulani thing and that all cattle understood the Fulani language.

In a way, such a belief was not far fetched because if we trace the cow Ali to its birth we shall find that it was very much Fulani. Firstly, the market where it was bought, although located in Balemba village, had cattle sellers who were all Fulani. They drove their cattle from their distant villages and brought them to the Balemba market. Ali in particular was born into a typical Fulani family, the Mustafa's. Ali's parents and grandparents were from Fulani families. That was as far as any living person could go with the cow's family tree.

Even so, there are high chances that generations far back were also Fulani.

So much was cattle rearing and obvious occupation for Fulani families that it was common for parents to keep children away from school so that they can help with looking after cattle. However, with government sensitization, the community throughout the country was beginning to wake up. Fulani elites were getting together and forming associations to fight Fulani marginalisation and get Fulani themselves to realise that education was the key to long-term success.

Nonetheless, it doubtful that as Ali the cow was given the two caretakers hard times on the bridge, he was even remotely thinking about the Fulani problem. Ali was simply reaching to a situation. For it, enough was enough and there was no way he was going to go beyond the bridge.

Finding that even insults in Fulani would not move Ali, Amungwa now lashed its back with a stick. As the cow define him by not budging, he rained more strokes on him until the stick got broke and he threw it away. But it had left weals on the cow's back. Yet, he did not move. Curing Amungwa pulled sharply several times on his own leash that was tied round the animal's hind foot. Still no respond. So, the foreman, Fundum pulled hard on his own leash, tied around the cow's neck, to make it move forward towards him. Still it did not work. At that point, Fundum had an idea. Passing his leash from his right to the left, he walked over to Ali, and stroking his neck affectionately, he said.

"Listen, Ali. If you think you are punishing us by digging in your heels, you are actually punishing everyone, including yourself. The longer you keep us here, the more tired we'll all become. So, just cut it out and let's go."

As if by magic, the cow relaxed and started walking forward.

"Yowa! Yowa!" shouted both Amungwa and Fundum in Fulani.

They both noticed that the cow was exhausted. It was still panting and was losing a lot of saliva through its open mouth. Here Amungwa felt that in a way, it was the animal's fault because while at the bridge when they had tried to lead it under the bridge for a drink of water, it had categorically refused not knowing that they were doing it a favour. It now he was thirsty, that was his problem because there would be no turning back.

Meanwhile at the college, Godlove was clearly getting impatient.

"This is not normal. Why has it taken so long for the cow to get here today? It's nearly two hours late."

"I hope they haven't mistakenly taken it to the village market, since today is a market day? It's easy because on a day like this several cows leave the cattle market for the village market where they are slaughtered and sold to butchers on the spot who then retail it to the market customers," said Brown the cook.

"Perhaps we ought to start thinking of what the students will have for lunch if that cow does not come in the end."

"I think so, chief."

"Okay, Brown, do we still have enough fish that can replace the meat just in case?"

"I'll go and look."

Upon that, Brown disappeared into the dining hall storeroom. Godlove removed his bunch of keys from his pocket, singled out a long and small key with which he started cleaning his teeth. Richard the steward who was watching him while peeling plantains at the washing up point situated on the side of the kitchen building suddenly remembered a story his junior brother who was at the St. Andrew's college told him. This story was about a classmate of the junior brother's who during a lesson had the rounded top of his pen break into his ear as he used it to clean his ear. When the poor boy tried to pull out the foreign body with the nib of the pen, he instead pushed it inside. He then started crying and the class teacher -the lesson was geography -took him to the principal who sent him to the hospital with a personal note for Dr. Rosenkeimer. The principal wrote:

Dear Dr. Roe.

    Please, kindly attend to this student with foreign body in his ear.

Regards.

Fr. Paul Lehman

Although it took the Doctor only seven minutes to extract the object with the sophisticated instrument his father had sent him from Bristol (England) the operation was very painful.

"You'll be alright. Just don't fool around with your ear any more. The ear is a very delicate part of the body."

"Yes Doctor. Thank you Doctor."

This was what Richard thought. Nonetheless, as he poured out the dirty water from the basin of peeled plantains, he shrugged his shoulders and said to himself.

"Anyway, that key is not a pen knob and Godlove is not the student who stuffed it into his ear."

****

By this time, the party of three, that is, the cow, the foreman and the hind man were approaching the urban part of the village, which was intersected by the high way that linked Mondamo Administrative Division to Bazongo Division. When approaching the centre of the urban area from the south, one found to the right, the road that led to the primary school, the cattle market and the village Fon's palace.

Another road that branched off to the left, led to the college and an agricultural station. At the angle between the northbound highway and the road leading to the village, there were, as there usually were everyday, women sited in an area a little larger than one half of a handball pitch. They called it a market. Normally, it looked too small to be called a market, but as far as they were concerned, it was a market, their market. They sold a wide range of foodstuffs: roasted groundnuts, ripe pears, bunches of plantains, ripe bananas, cola nuts, sugarcane. Nearby, there was a butcher's slab. He was a middle-aged man called Pa Bone, because he sold soft bone that many buyers loved.

"Gafara! Gafara!" shouted the hind man as the three galloped down towards the "market." As they did so, the angry, tired, fuming cow trotted as if it would kill anyone in its way.

Some people, saying how fierce the cow looked, quickly stepped away from the earthen and wet road and took cover in the nearby corn farms, or plantain farms or coffee farms, as the case might be.

However, some two boys, in their attractive light blue shirts and khaki shorts that were the uniform of the village Catholic school, suddenly stopped unto the middle of the road, and in full view of the approaching cow, made the death-to-you sign and stamped their feet on the road to emphasize their death sentence. As if stung, the cow leaped at them, taking both the hind man and the foreman by surprise. In the struggle to regain their balance, both men fell to the ground, but being as die-hard as Spartans, they hung on to their leashes. The result was that as the cow chased the boys, it dragged both men along, off the road and unto the nearby farms. At some point they lost their grip and the cow continued along leading foreman and moaning and writhing in pain. In their panic, the two schoolboys fell over the farm ridges several times, staining their school bags. Unfortunately for the cow, the two boys disappeared as they hid in a nearby thicket.

A bit calmer now, the cow continued its journey, although it is doubtful whether it really knew where it was going or whether it remembered at this point whom it had been chasing in the first place. It walked over and across the groundnut and corn farm, smashing ridges, distorting their form and killing sprouting crops. It was certain that the poor woman whose farm it was would curse the animal on finding its hoof marks. But what would it matter, since the cow would be gone anyway?

Ali the cow came across a side road and took it. Fortunately it found no one on the way. As there were no farm beds to impede its movements, quicken its pace and soon broke into a run. The side road led into the village road from which the schoolboys had diverted the cow. As it entered the road, a group of market goers screamed: "Cow, oh!"

And ran helter skelter. Some onlookers who have seen the incident involving the two boys quickly ran towards the direction where the cow was. But it was now heading towards the small market located at the angle. Before it got there, saleswomen who saw the unmanned cow were in disarray. They all got up and ran helter skelter, some screaming and calling the names of their late parents or grandparents. One said in English. "I am covered with the blood of Jesus!" Some fell over others and were trampled upon, although not to death.

The cow now entered the highway. It could have turned right to go up towards Bazungo Division, or straight ahead towards the agricultural station or even towards the college for whose students it had been bought. But the cow instead went left and down the highway towards the village market. Towards the north the highway was steep for about a kilometre and south where the cow was heading, it was down hill for about two kilometres. It probably chose this route because it was easiest going down dale. So, it followed the line of least resistance, the primitive path.

So down the road went the mad cow, saliva dripping from his mouth. Now that he was on the tarred highway, its hoofs made its galloping sound so loud that people could hear it before it came into view. Of course some mistook the hoof echoes for those of a horse, horse not being uncommon in the village. The reaction was the same. As soon as people realized it was a loose cow, they scrambled out of sight for cover.

From where the cow and that was half way between the women's makeshift market and the main market, there were practically no more provocative pupils still walking to school. This was because they were already at school. So, the cow was spared any more taunts.

When it got to the part of the highway that passed just in front of the highway, it scared the many people, there, some of whom were haggling others buying and others about to board waiting taxis. Yet some had their private cars. Some

22

others, notably women, stood in groups, greeting and chatting. As the cow came closer, people scattered in all directions. Then it suddenly found that it was caught between the parked vehicles on the left and right and a line of some three vehicles approaching it from down. Instinctively, it stood still. Then the driver of the vehicle right in front of him, probably impatient of waiting, probably nervous or even frightened, let out a long and piercing hoot on his horn. Frightened, too, the cow leaped over one of the cars and made a dash into the market.

Here all hell broke loose, for the entire market was in total confusion. The cow ran about wildly, knocking people and things down. Some victims cried out for help, others started weeping and exclaiming in their mother tongue, people ran wild with some just running because they saw others doing so. The cow even ran into njangi huts and market bars, breaking some down. The biggest victim was Pa Awantang whose hut was partly damaged, his jugs and calabashes of njangi palm wine broken, njangi members in panic as they tried to run, unconscious of where they were going. The cow got out of the hut and unfortunately for one mother, her 11 years old son was running towards the cow without noticing it. Before the mother attempted to rescue her child, the cow had picked him up with his horns and hurled him unto open large bags of garri. He was not hurt. By this time, it appeared the entire market had known there was something wrong. So in loud singular chorus, they booed, the way they always did when it had rained and was slippery and someone slipped and fell in the market.

As everyone was scared of the cow and making way for it, it ran towards the back of the market and exited through the gap between the butchers' slap and the second hand clothes section. It then entered a nearby a corn farm and started ploughing through it. Some men and boys gave chase. Because of the ridges of the corn beds, the animal's movement was inhibited and because the chasers were pressurizing it, it soon fell and as a result of its large size, it

23

could not get up quickly. The pursuers pounced upon it with sticks and stones. Some five minutes later, it stopped movement apart from breathing.

"Don't kill it, please! Don't, please!" That was the foreman, followed closely by the hind man. Both were tearing through the huge crowd that had gathered round the animal. The two men then explained to the other people what had happened.

"If we don't slaughter it at once, it will die out of exhaustion and the blows. And if it dies, there is no way it can be slaughtered. The veterinary assistants will not allow anyone eat meat from an animal that dies before slaughter."

With the consent of the two herdsmen, the butchers went to work. They were three and within twenty minutes, they had finished the job.

The hind man took a chance, not knowing what the chief cook at the college would say, and gave the butchers the head, the skin, the tail and legs. They paid some idle boys a little money and they transported the meat on their heads to the college.

The kitchen staff looked lost when they saw nine heads in all bringing parts of a slaughtered cow to the refectory. When the hind man narrated the story to Godlove the chief cook, he said.

"I knew there was something wrong."

"Didn't I tell you, Brown?"

The question for Brown was more or less a rhetorical one.

"Okay, wait here, I'll go and tell the principal what has happened."

When he told the principal, the latter said to him:

"We have only an hour left for the students' lunch. Have you prepared something else for them to eat in place of meat?"

"Yes, sir. There is fish."

"Is it ready?"

"Yes, Sir."

24

"Fine prepare fish for lunch and the cow for supper. I don't see anything wrong with that."

"Yes Sir."

3

Wrong foot forward

Peter Ngwa Akuma was well known in Azope town, the divisional headquarters of Kulanja. A tax officer for many years, he worked in several parts of the country before being posted to Azope as divisional chief of service for taxation. He worked in Azope for five years before being put on retirement. Once he was posted there where incidentally he had not worked before, he made up his mind that he would stay in Azope with his family after retiring. Peter Ngwa Akuma was not a native of Azope neither was he even from Kulanja division. In fact, he was from Mbome in Nyen division, hence the name, Akuma. His mother though was from Batuf, which was why he was named, Ngwa, after his material grandfather. For anyone who understood the socio-political map of the country, Menam, was no surprise that Peter chose this locality for his retirement home. Right from independence in the early 1960s, the government had adopted a policy by which it posted any civil servant, at anytime, to any part of the country. It is worth pointing out that the country had over two hundred national languages in addition to French and English being the official ones. The result was that even in a divisional headquarters like Azope one could find oneself living and working side-by-side with compatriots from many other parts of the country. In terms of the official languages, such postings and working arrangements meant that entire families which had moved into a zone where the other official language dominated, could learn and beginning to use it fairly easily within a couple of years. For Peter and his living in Azope, that official language vantage point was irrelevant because Kulanja, just like his own administrative division, Nyen, was in the predominantly English speaking part of the country. However, his family, including the children, spoke French, the reason being that he had served in French-speaking towns before, although not in the capital.

Peter Ngwa Akuma and his wife, Akuma Bernadette, née Ambe, had five children, two of whom left the Ecole Normal Superieure and were now secondary school teachers. The eldest, Diana, taught English at the Lycée de Bangoualenga and her immediate junior, Louisa, was an Economics teacher at the Government High School (GHS), Bissouma. They were aged 32 and 28 respectively. Although Louisa was happily married with four children, Diana was still searching. Occasionally, she joked with friends saying if she hit 40 without finding a man, she would give up getting married altogether. Roman, aged 25 was in the United States of America, having been helped over by a cousin of his out there in Wisconsin. He was doing business administration, or so, his parents were told. Justus, 21, was a second year law student at the University of Benka, the national capital. The Benjamin of the family, Sandine, was aged 18 and in the Upper Sixth at Azope Government Bilingual High school (GBHS). Mrs. Akuma herself was headmistress of the local Government Nursery School. She was part of the first batch of candidates who entered the Ecole Normale Superieure for training Grade One teachers. After graduating, she taught in a government primary school and was later appointed chief of service in charge of teacher administration at the Ngwambong sub inspectorate of primary and nursery education. It was from there that she was appointed headmistress of Government Nursery School Azope. Two years before her husband went on retirement, she remarked to him that she was four years from it. She said it would be her greatest wish to set up her own nursery school in Azope, the idea being that nursery education was her sector. Besides, there was only one nursery school in the town, yet the population was growing. Thirdly, Mrs. Akuma just fell in love with the town and its people. She enjoyed the plain landscape of the region and liked the smiling and accommodating disposition of the people. Here, both she and her husband vibrated on the same wavelength because he had also fallen in love with Azope hence his decision to make the town his dream retirement home. At the time Bernadette's husband retired, he had built the much dreamed about home, in a quiet and forward-looking district of Azope. He had not finished construction work. However, work had advanced well enough for him and his family to move into the house. It was a modern, ambitious five bed roomed house, overlooking an expanded hilltop with a sweet singing steam below that separated that hill from the other one. In the wee hours of the morning when the atmosphere was calm and the family still in bed, the croaking of frogs and the light splashing and echoing of the nearby stream produced a sweet music which no one could ignore, but which Akuma's household and their neighbours took for granted, familiarity having bred contempt.

Akuma had managed to roof the house, fit all door and window shutters. Unfortunately, he was able to plaster just the sitting room, the bedrooms, kitchen and toilets having to wait until he got the first lump sum payment of his pension. It must be said that the new house was a major improvement on his previous home, which was rented property. This one was made of cement blocks whereas the previous one was built of sun dried bricks. The new house had two more bedrooms than the previous one. Over and above everything else was the comfort that he was now living in his own house. His wife was equally proud.

The only snag is that to get that far, Akuma had to use his savings and even borrow the Credit Union. His wife chipped in something, though. He was never despondent, knowing that he no longer had to pay rents to anyone. Besides, he knew that once he received his lump sum, it would go a long way towards redressing the balance.

****

A couple of months after Akuma and his family moved into the new house, he and his wife decided that he should travel to the capital, to see what was delaying payment of his lump sum. This was because no service at the divisional or the provincial level gave the impression that they could do anything to speed up the treatment of his dossier. The process was complicated and involved different ministerial departments such as the public service, territorial administration and finance. Although the ministry under which he worked was Finance, that did not make life any easier for him. Once he went to the divisional chief of taxes for Kulanja for a letter of recommendation to take to Yaounde, but the divisional chief referred him to his own boss, the provincial chief. When he went to the provincial chief, he was most unhelpful because his only reaction was, "Mr. Akuma. You know that retirement dossiers are not treated at the provincial level. You must go to Benka. Everything happens in the capital. The government has for decades talked about decentralisation. But if they have not empowered us to treat your dossiers at our level, what do you expect us to do?"

So, poor Akuma left for Benka and went straight to the house of a cousin of his who was a chief of service in the Ministry of Transport. He got to Benka on a Sunday evening. His host, wife and children were happy to see him, or so they said. Before he went to bed, he asked his cousin, very much a Benka man, how to go about chasing his money.

"Check with your ministry, Finance. Find out from personnel where exactly your dossier is. I hope you brought some money to tip the people you will be coming across?"

"I have some money. I brought some, not much, but I brought it."

"Well, that's something. Money is the only language these people understand."

Akuma went to the door marked "Chef du Service Personnel" and knocked. As he got no reply, he kept

29

knocking. Abruptly, someone opened the door and barked at him like a dog.

"Qu'est-ce que vous voulez?" he asked in French.

"I want to see the Chief of Personnel," he replied calmly and politely

"Je ne parle pas votre anglais-là. Qu'est-ce que vous voulez, Monsieur?"

"I want to see the personnel chief," answered Akuma in the same manner. As he did so, he was saying to himself that if this man's objective were to intimidate him into speaking French, then he would fail. Why could the man not also speak to him in English? Was English not as much an official language in this country as French?"

The official told him rudely in French that he was a Chief of Service with a secretariat and a secretary. If he wanted to see him, he must go through the secretariat next door.

Akuma understood and complied. He understood French. In fact, he spoke French after having served in some French speaking towns. His problem was not speaking French. It was being forced into speaking it, even when he freely opted to speak English. The constitution of the country allowed for two official languages but did not impose any of the two on anyone or any group of people. So why should he be forced to speak French? The secretary offered him a sit, unexpectedly, and then asked him what was the problem. When he told her it was the payment of his pension, she advised him that in that case, he was wasting his time coming to the personnel service of the Ministry of Finance. He spoke English to her and he spoke French to him.

"But I was a Ministry of Finance employee."

"I know. But that's not how it works. You have to go the personnel service of the Ministry of Public service. That is where your file is supposed to be."

Akuma thanked her and as he walked to the door, he thought about how the woman was so different from his boss. Should he not give her something for a beer? Finally, he turned round, got out his wallet and was about to give her two thousand francs when he realised that he only had a five thousand note and a five hundred francs note. Reluctantly, he gave her the five hundred francs note but was taken aback by how appreciative the woman was. In fact, if one had to judge by the extent of her joy, one would think she had been given five thousand francs and not five hundred francs. He once more thanked her and left.

Peter reasoned that since it was ten minutes past three (and closing time) there was little point in going to public service. So, he decided to return home and come back the following day.

The following morning Akuma reported at the public service personnel department. But this time he went to the secretariat of the chief of service, not the chief of service himself, having learned his lesson.

When he knocked at the door, the reply was very loud and unfriendly:

"Oui, entrez!"

He opened the door respectfully, one would say, apologetically and stood before the secretary: She sized him up for about a minute. Within her, she reasoned that this man who came in looking lost and not even wearing a coat and tie was certainly a lightweight.

"Qu'est-ce que vous voulez ici? Vous entrez et vous ne saluez même pas les gens!"

"No, that's not true. I greeted you. I said good morning madam!"

"Good morning, c'est quoi? c'est ça qu'on mange?"

"No, madam, I was not offering you my good morning as a meal, so I didn't expect you to eat it as you put it."

"Ça va. Vous voulez quoi?"

Akuma painstakingly explained about his file, after which the woman nonchalantly said: "Mais le chef n'est pas là. Repassez dans une semaine."

"Next week, madam? No, that's too long. I can't wait for a whole week."

"Dans ce cas, parlez bien alors et je vais voir ce que je peux faire."

"What do you mean by I should speak well and you will see what you can do?"

The secretary now continued in pidgin after laughing at Akuma's ignorance.

"You no be man for this country? Put hand for pocket and give me something."

"Give you something like what, madam?"

"Two thousand francs will do. She continued in French. "By the way, your file is not with the Chief. I can trace it and get to the exact office. But that will take some time and a little more effort on your part. If you like, you can "fix" me and just come back for the result in three working days. If the file has to be taken to another office or service, I will still help you."

Akuma felt the message was very clear. So he gave her the sum of FCFA5,000, out of desperation since he needed to have things done.

With the money, the woman was all smiles and even spoke some English for the first time. "Is no problem. Come back here in three day…Three days! Thank you!"

When Akuma returned to his cousin's place, he was exhausted. So, to his cousin's question about whether his file was progressing, he simply said: "Yes."

"Where exactly is the file now?"

"At personnel in the Public Service."

"That sounds alright."

When Akuma returned to public service on the appointed day, the woman told him that she had made enquiries and knew where the file was.

"My brother who works in that service will come and take you there and then help you."

She dialled her table telephone and spoke to someone in a national language he could not place.

"Il arrive! Asseyez vous!"

32

"You mean your brother is already coming to collect me?"

"Yes!"

A few minutes later, a neatly dressed man in a charcoal gray suit and tie came in.

"That's him," said the secretary.

Meanwhile, Akuma wondered why each time he came into that office, he never saw the chief of service. Yet, next to the secretary, he could see his door label: "Chef du personnel."

He never heard him call her from inside, neither did he see him coming out or going in. The secretary never entered or left his office. Anyway, as Akuma left with the secretary's so called brother, he shrugged his shoulders and thought to himself: "Well, that's not what matters now."

His "guide," so to speak, was a flamboyant man who could be in his late thirties. He seemed to know the ministry well. But Akuma felt he was stopping too many times to enter one office or another or to chat with Akuma in the corridor, saying "Une minute!"

But he was away for a good half hour, during which Akuma was pestered, harassed and pressurized by some equally well-dressed young men who prowled the corridors, apparently in search for someone. They told him they could help him with any problem in the public service ministry or even the ministry of Finance. They spoke fluent French and English. They told him after he talked about his problem that with the sum of FCFA50,000, they could have his pension dossier treated. With another FCFA50,000, they could get his lump sum paid within a week. If he wanted the monthly pension to be activated the following month, he would simply have to add another FCFA50,000.

"But I don't have money," pleaded Akuma

"No problem. Where are you from?"

"The North West."

"No problem. Give us the first FCFA50,000 to start the process, and then you go to Bamenda and look for the rest of

33

the money. We are the only ones who can do this thing for you, and do it in record time.

Just then, the door opened and Akuma's "guide" came out. As soon as Akuma's companions saw him, they quickly hurried away.

"Les salauds!" he exclaimed giving them a dirty look. "Be careful, those men are not good."

He and Akuma got to an office whose locked door was unmarked.

"It's here," he told Akuma. "Wait outside!" Without knocking, the man went in and locked the door before him. Shortly after, he came out.

"They are asking for FCFA2,000," he informed Akuma.

"They who?" "The people who have your file."

"What is the money for?"

"It's for the file search."

"But I gave your sister FCFA50,000 for all this."

"Yes it was my sister who referred you to me and I brought you here, so you can't accuse her of anything."

"No! no! I'm not. Here is the money."

"They say you should come back in a week"

"What! A week? Why? I can't wait for a week. My money is finished and my family back at home needs me."

"Okay, no problem. Can you add another FCFA10,000 and come back tomorrow or FCFA5,000 and come back in three days?"

"That is scandalous! This is bribery and corruption which is a crime."

"No, it's not. You want a quick service and that's how you can get it. Do you think you are the only one with files in this ministry? I'm just trying to help you."

Akuma felt very hurt and abused. But he knew he had no choice.

"Okay, I'll come back in a week's time."

****

When Peter returned the week later, he managed to trace the office to which his guide had taken him. But since he had not entered the office, its occupants claimed not to understand his problem. They also said there was nobody like the one he was describing working in that office. With assistance from people he found on his way, he finally went back to the personnel office to find out exactly what was going on from the secretary.

"Madam, where is your brother? We had an appointment today?"

"Ah! Did he not get you the file last week?"

"No. It's today we were supposed to meet."

"Okay. Hold on!" She picked up her phone, again chatted with someone in her language. After she put down the phone she announced to Akuma: "He went to the village. He lost his brother."

"What! So, when is he coming back, Madam?"

"I don't know," she said in a very detached manner." But I think you should wait for him to return."

"My God! Wait for a man when I don't know when he is coming?"

****

Akuma spent the next five months in the capital, being tossed in that manner like a volley ball. Back in Azope, his wife had exhausted all sources of financial assistance: bank, njangis friends etc. In Yaounde, his host family, after speaking to him in coded language to no avail, was now gently asking him to go and live somewhere else.

"When you just arrived, we thought it was for a couple of weeks. But you have been here for nearly six months. Life here is very difficult," said his cousin's wife.

"Denise is right, Peter," concurred her husband. Peter could not believe what he heard. If Denise was pushing him out, he could understand it. But not his cousin! They had grown up together in the village. In fact, they had so much in common that he did not think it was Anselm who could do that to him. But alas, there was the harsh reality. After thinking very hard, he plucked courage and said to Anselm: "Do you know that I don't even have money to return home?"

"Don't worry, Peter, I'll lend you the fare."

"Oh, thank you, brother!" Peter said repeatedly. Although he was disappointed with his cousin, he felt that this last ditch offer was commendable. And so, the following day, Peter returned to Azope, a dejected, absent-minded man who had lost a lot of weight and looked sick.

As soon as his wife saw him, she ran to him and hugged him:

"Oh my God! What has happened to you! You look different! Were you starving while in Benka?"

"Oh! Don't even ask Ben, I have simply been to hell and back."

****

The Akuma family was from then on plugged into a crisis. Life became very difficult, there was no more money to return to the capital and chase the pension dossier. Even when someone fell ill, there was never enough money to buy drugs, Akuma's wife was stretched to the fullest and those had lent her money were now making her life miserable. She and her husband for the first time wrote to Roman in American to send some money, but got no replies. Diana and her junior sister Louisa provided whatever assistance they could. But good intentioned as the gesture was, it all amounted to nothing more than a drop in the ocean. Things got to a point where Peter said he would sell the unfinished house and the plot so that they could go back to renting.

"No, my dear husband! That would be capitulation and we would become a laughing stock in this town."

And so the cavalry continued. The following year, Justus who now doing his Maîtrise degree in law but who could not return to university because his parents had neither the FCFA50,000 tuition fee, no money for his room and board, surprised them all. On a Friday night, he woke everyone at about 3 o'clock at night to say he was feeling unwell. Throughout that day, and in fact that week and month, he had been in top from. His parents gave him some paracetamol tablets and he returned to bed. An hour later, when his father went to his bedroom to see how he was doing, he found the young man to be sweating profusely, although he was not under the blanket. His body was very hot. His father also noticed his son was having difficulty breathing.

"Ben! Ben!"

"Yes, dear!" His wife came rushing out of their bedroom.

"We must take Justus to the hospital."

By this time Justus was unconscious because he could not even answer his mother calling him repeatedly. They managed to find a taxi. Unfortunately, before they reach the hospital, Justus died on the way.

His death was a surprise to everyone, including his two teaching sister, Diana and Louisa who wondered how it could have happened so abruptly when thy never heard their brother was ill.

Letters sent to Roman in America about his brother's death were still not answered. The parents and his two elder sisters each wrote again. Still, there was no reply. It was clear now that they did not know where Roman was. So, it looked to them as though they had lost him.

Justus' death was a big blow to the family, with every single member feeling that something irreplaceable had gone away. Even Sandrine, the Benjamin of the family, also now at home because she could not return to university where she had enrolled after her Advanced levels, felt that the loss of Justus was devastating.

However, the blow of the sledgehammer was felt more by Justus' father. Although Peter always endeavoured not to show it, he had a small spot for Justus, among all his children. Secretly he had chosen him as his next of king. So, from where did this injustice come, taking father before son? By a trust of faith, Justus also resembled his father physically more than any of the other children. The death affected Akuma psychologically. He now became absent-minded, ate little, talked little and was forgetful. His wife worried about him and would occasionally tell the children: "Talk to your father."

Although the Akuma family had not been great church goers, these troubles brought the charismatic movement of the Catholic Church, the Catholic Men's Association (CMA), the Catholic Women's Association (CWA) and other prayer groups nearer them.

But since it never rains but it pours, Sandrine died the following year, hit by a vehicle in the town itself. She was walking along the main road with three friends, with vehicles speeding past as they always did. Suddenly they heard people shouting in pidgin: "Wuna run! Wuna run!"

When the girls turned round, they found that a truck laden with stones, apparently for the construction of a house, had veered off the road and was coming towards them. They took off helter skelter. In the process, the vehicle caught one of the girls. And it was Sandrine who died on the spot. When the news got to her home and her father heard it, he fainted. Fanning and dowsing with water brought him to. Even so, he completely lost his speak faculty.

After the burial, he started behaving strangely. He could sit on one spot for four hours without getting up. He also started failing to understand human speech, in addition to being unable to sit up.

One morning, he got up at about five in the morning, went out as if he was going to the toilet and then did not return until the following morning. Surprisingly, he was now speaking, although his speech lacked coordination. He would say things like: "Yes, I hit him on the head, that dirty priest. Why did he take my tax forms?"

Peter stopped eating "proper" food, claiming that since nobody could cook well, he was now coking for himself. He would remove his shoes and be seen walking barefooted in the town. He started saying he could not sleep in the house because it was too hot.

"Where will you sleep, then?"

"Outside. In the yard."

"In open air? At this hour? It is 11 p.m. dear!" exclaimed the wife.

But Peter had switched on to something else. He was saying:

"You mad man! Why do you think I am here" I am looking for my pension dossier. I walked from Bamenda to here, Douala. Is that the Minister? But I told him his car had been stolen. Ha! Ha! Ha!"

Overwhelmed, Bernadette started crying: "My dear husband! What has happened to you" You are talking to yourself!"

Peter looked surprised. Shortly after he pulled the bedroom mattress out into the yard, took one pillow and a blanket and lay alone in the middle of the yard at that late hour.

Oh my God! Dear, if that is where you will spend the night, we must spend it there together," his wife said going back into the bedroom to fetch the other pillow.

As she walked towards him lying in that incongruous position, it started raining heavily. It didn't bother him because he instead tucked himself away on the mattress and started snoring.

"No! Mother, you can't! You shouldn't!" said Diana and Louisa who happened to be around. It was holidays. As they urged their mother, they were pulling her away from the rain.

"But how about him? How about him?" she asked exasperatedly. She burst into tears again, her daughters weeping with her. There was nothing they could do about the husband and father.

Two hours later, the rain ceased as abruptly as it had started. Surprisingly, Peter got up, drenched but not shivering. His daughters pulled the mattress back into the house to dry it. The blanket and pillowcases were washed.

Their father allowed himself to bathed and clad by his wife. She improvised a mattress and they went to bed. But when she got up at 5 p.m. her husband had gone.

Diana, have you seen your father?"

"No, mother. Is he not with you?"

"He was. We slept here together as you will remember. But now he isn't here."

Peter disappeared for three days. Later that day, a family friend who had come in from   Bamenda said he saw Peter some six villages away, barefooted, unwashed, unshaved, wearing dirty and stained clothes. He was picking up ants from the street and eating them. When he asked Peter what he was doing there, his reply was:

"God's work. I am doing God's work."

Then he opened a large black plastic bag in which he appeared to have his belongings, took out a track and showed it to the family friend. It said: "Repent, for the time has come!"

What puzzled the man was whether in such a state Peter could do any preaching.

The church groups were very supportive of Peter's family, or what remained of it. They prayed together, sang together and shared the little they had, including food and money.

One day, at mass, the priest singled out the Akuma family as a typical example of a Christian family that had gone through thick and thin. It had bowed but had not been broken.

"Have faith, brothers and sisters. Trust in God for he has told us he is the way, the life and the truth. It is all right for us to love someone but we must make allowance for God's intervention in whatever way he deems fit. He can choose whatever way he wants to take us. He can take us dead or alive. I believe he has taken Peter alive. That is why although no one feeds him, he is still alive and strong. God looks after him. I want to ask Bernadette and the children and, in fact, the entire congregation, to consider that Peter is gone. He is no longer with us. God is a great father who can speak to us in a million ways. Perhaps Peter was needed as that scapegoat that God would use to tell this government that there is something seriously wrong with its workings. The government is so corrupt that an honest man like Peter cannot have his pension to which he is entitled. Instead, he has to bribe at every corner, get indebted, watch his children die one after the other, and then go mad himself. Let us pray that the government learns a lesson and sanitizes the system. Amen."

Peter was never seen again.

4

Lost In London City

The sharp shutting of the door mail flap woke Martha. At once she knew it was the postman. She got up quickly and looked out of the window of the bedroom that overlooked the main road. She and caught a glimpse of him removing some more mail from the side bags of his bicycle and going towards her neighbour's house.

The sharp closure of the flap had been immediately followed by the thud of postal deliveries being dropped on the carpet inside of the front door. As Martha went downstairs, many thoughts came to her mind. Was it one letter or two? Was there any junk mail included? Oh! These bastards of firms who think they know too much. They "steal" people's postal addresses from whatever source and then pester them with letters offering all kinds of products or services. The problem is that even when you do not want them it is not easy to get them off your back. Martha also wondered whether she would find any letters from home, from her family. Was all well at home? She wondered.

She found five letters on the floor. Two were precisely junk mail, one was her telephone bill, and another electricity bill and the fifth, from her parent back in Baligham written by her mother. Martha decided to open the letter from home last, because she was sure that whether was the case, it would throw her off balance. Either someone was in desperate need of money, or was seriously ill or had even died. There were times when the same letter announced up to three deaths. Oh, these letters from home!

She did not even bother to open the junk mail. She put it straight in the dustbin. Her telephone bill was high, so disconcerting that she went to the sitting room before analysing it. She could not take the blow standing. Eight hundred and fifty pounds! Well, she was expecting a high bill, but not that high. The fact is that being a very careful and responsible girl, she was not really the one who ran up such a huge bill. Four months ago, an uncle of hers (a junior brother to her father) who was in London from Cameroon for business, spent two weeks with her in her Finsbury Park flat. She had authorised him to make some calls but never expected such a bill. Unfortunately, her uncle left saying as soon as he got back to Douala, he would send her the money. It was now four months and she had not heard a word from him neither had he sent the money. British Telecom gave Martha two weeks within which if she did not settle her bill, she would be cut off.

Her electricity bill was not unduly high, but still, it was a bill to be paid, because it still meant money going out. For that one, she also had a two-week deadline. "Oh what a life!" she said to herself. Yet, back at home, everyone seems to think that here in the Whiteman's country, we all swim ion money.

By the time she got to the letter from her mother, her head felt like it was swelling inside. She plucked courage and tore open the envelope. After glancing at the letter, she leapt up stung.

"What! I don't believe this! Can my mother really say this to me about me? That I neglect her? I don't send her money? O my God! O my God! I don't believe this!"

In her grief, she perhaps unconsciously clasped the letter and ran upstairs crying. In the bedroom, she flung herself on the bed and wept bitterly. She was too overcome by distress to continue reading the letter. In fact, she did not want to see it any more. So, she opened her bedside drawer, stuffed it inside and keyed the drawer.

All of a sudden, she remembered she had to iron her boyfriend's clothes quickly and prepare herself for college. For all of that the time at her disposal was only 45 minutes. She forced herself to stop crying.

What made Martha feel so bad was not only that her mother had unexpectedly made a U-turn and accused her of neglect. It was also the fact that life in Britain was exceedingly difficult, very far removed from what people at home thought it was.

What kind of country was this where all of one's earnings were swallowed up by bills and one had to borrow more in order to survive, with the result being that one was more indebted? Strictly speaking, Martha was simply patching up in London, so to speak. She had gone to the British capital as a government-sponsored student of her country, Cameroon. That was when the economic situation was bright. Having scored good marks in Mathematics, Chemistry, Physics and Biology, the government awarded her a scholarship to study for a BSc in Environmental Management. Cameroon's career planners felt students like Martha, if possible, go on to do a research degree in that discipline so that when they returned home, they could use their expertise to bolster the newly created Ministry of the Environment and Forestry. So, she did the BSc successfully at Bromington University. She went on to do the MSc in Environmental Waste Management at the same university. Unfortunately, just as she was making arrangements to go on to the PhD degree, the economic crisis set in and her home government found it difficult to continue sponsoring the over 500 students in Britain, the cost of whose university education for foreign students was known to be one of the highest in Europe. There began Martha's litany of woes. Her scholarship was scraped, which meant no more tuition fee, no living allowances. After she continued to live in the university hostel for months without being able to pay rents, the university authorities, tied of promises to pay that never bore fruit, threw her out. That was three weeks before the nasty letter from her mother arrived.

When Martha lost her place in the university hall of residence, a friend of her's from Ghana too her into her flat. It was a Council flat. Council flats were popular because they were good value for money. Perpetua, Martha's friend had a two-bedroom flat in a well located part of Finsbury Park, a part of London very popular among African residents, perhaps because it had their favourite items such as foodstuffs: cocoyam, palm oil, garri, pepper, okro eru, fufu corn, beans, yam, treated cow legs, gizzard and all kinds of condiments. In fact, Finsbury Park was like a slice of Africa in London. Although it was not the only such African "island" in the British capital, it was a blessing for people like Martha who lived nearby.

As far as mobility was concerned, Perpetua's flat was just ten minutes' walk from the Finsbury Park underground railway station. The underground network was so good in terms of rapidity that once on it, on could get to any other part of London. To go into the heart of London, Perpetua and Martha would just walk to the tube station. However, when they were pressed for time, they would hop on one of London's double decked buses.

Perpetua gave Martha one of the two bedrooms and lived in the other. They shared a kitchen, living room and toilet/bathroom. The council charged thirty pounds for rents excluding rates, which in British parlance meant water and electricity. In turn, Perpetua charged her sub-tenant twenty pounds which when paid, she simply added another ten pounds to arrive at the thirty pounds the Council expected. Martha was happy about the arrangement because without it, she would be out on the streets like a tramp or even a prostitute. As she used to tell Perpetua when thanking her, when she was homeless, none of her compatriots accepted to offer her shelter. Some said they did not have any room, although as she put it, she knew they did. Others said they had been betrayed enough by people they tried to help who ended up by contacting the immigration police and telling lies about them, which lies led the police harassing them with deportation. In fact, as soon as Martha was thrown out of her university room, she first packed into the flat of a cousin of hers, Valerie. And she did so without prior notice.

When she rang Valerie's doorbell and she opened the door, her immediate reaction on seeing her was: "Oh my

God! Martha, what are you doing here? And I see you have brought your things!"

"It's bad, Valerie. Very bad. The university has thrown me out of my room."

"Why?"

"For owing seven months of rents."

"Seven months! But that's a lot of money."

"You know the situation of us government-sponsored students."

"Yes, I know." And she did, because Valerie also went to Britain as a government-sponsored student. Fortunately for her, she was of an earlier generation. So, she was able to earn her PhD and get a job as a researcher for a baby food manufacturing company on the outskirts of London. She was fairly well to do and settled. She went to work in her own car, unless she deliberately decided to travel by train. She earned a good salary and was now thinking of moving out of her Council flat into her own house. Already, she had contacted a number of housing agencies. Once she found her dream house in a good location, she would get a mortgage and buy it. The only vacuum in Valerie's life for now was a husband. She did not have a husband. For now she was dating a Nigerian insurance broker but found him to be too much of an adventurer who was always evasive when she raised the issue of marriage. Valerie's flat was passed on to her by a Sierra Leonian university mate of hers who had British nationality because she was born in London. So, it was easier for her, a British citizen, to get s council flat.

When she bought her house, she rang Valerie and offered her the three-bed roomed flat, on condition that she never defaulted on payment of results. If she did, the council might start asking too many questions and find out that she was not the rightful owner. On the other hand, if she paid regularly, no eyebrows would be raised. That was what Valerie's friend wanted because although she had given out the flat, she still wanted it to remain hers.

46

Now that Valerie was looking for her own place, she could easily have recommended Martha to her friend. But she did not. As she was fond of saying, she did not like involving family members in serious matters because they always ended up doing the wrong things, most of the times deliberately in order to spite you, instead of thanking you. Valerie did not even tell her cousin she was soon going to buy a house.

For now, what concerned her was Martha's intrusion this early morning. She asked Martha after they had moved her things in and sat down in the living room:

"Why didn't you phone before coming?"

"You know my situation, Valerie."

"Your situation? What situation, Martha? How much does it cost to make a phone call? What if you didn't find me in?"

"God would have allowed that to happen."

"God? What has God to do with it?"

"I mean... I..."

"Oh come on, Martha... By the way, what are your plans? You know you can't stay here."

"I know. If you can give me some time to find a place and something to do, I will be grateful."

"How? You have no money to find a place to live. You have no work permit to look for a job. If anything you are an illegal immigrant, now that the Cameroon government and the university have abandoned you."

"I know, Valerie. I will look for a cleaning job somewhere. There are thousands of African girls and boys here in London who are doing cleaning jobs. As for a place to live, God will provide."

"Well, you better ask God to provide fast because I give you seven days to be in this flat. It is not mine and my friend gave me strict instructions not to let anyone live here, either for rent or free of charge."

Martha knew her cousin was just looking for a way of getting rid of her because although Valerie's boy friend had a place of his, he was literally living in Valerie's flat. In fact, he spent ninety per cent of his time there. So, why had Valerie's friend not objected to that? Anyway, Martha concluded to herself that such intricacies would not deter her in the search for stability in her life. In the days that followed, she did her best to look for both a place to live and a clearing job. Finally, she was made a job offer in an office around the Euston Square area. She was given an office that she had to clean between 5am and 7am every weekday, thus giving users enough time before they started arriving. Her supervisor, a certain Mrs. Sally Green, introduced her to the office security guards. She was to collect the key from the guards and return it to them after finishing.

Early morning office cleaning was the easiest job for foreign immigrants like Martha whose residential status in the UK was irregular. In her case, her stay had expired two years earlier, which was a very serious immigration offence. If found out, there was no doubt she would be deported, which meant being taken by surprise when she least expected it. She would be grabbed and driven straight to the airport. She would then be forcefully sat in a waiting plane with a policeman sitting on either side of her.

Once the plane landed in her country, she would then be pushed out, literally: "Good riddance!"

Accounts of deportation abounded and were well known, especially in the African Community. Africans were the ones who bore the brunt of it. It is not clear whether their black colour made them easy targets or whether there was in the United Kingdom, a general belief that because Africa was a poor continent, its citizens were looking for every conceivable excuse to come to Britain and then do everything to stay.

One day, a Ghanaian family; living on the fourth floor of a Council Estate, received a knock at the door.

"Who is it?" asked the father of the house, Kwame Kwesi.

"The Police!", came the reply from those knocking.

At once, Kwame was seized by terror. Not knowing what to do, as his stay had expired ten years ago and he managed to stay in the system undetected, he was convinced that today the game was up. The immigration police net had closed in on him and there was no hiding. Incidentally, his entire family of seven children and a wife was home that Saturday early morning. The entire family knew his situation and they feared even all the more that if the father of the home got in trouble, they would not be spared. They were all standing, troubled and confused.

Bang! Bang! Bang! Came the police again: "Is there anyone in this flat?"

In a flash, Kwame opened the window and jumped out and so went down four floors. Down below, the crash of his landing immediately drew the attention of other residents of the estate, including children playing in the yard.

Kwame's family watching from the fourth floor window was in tears because even from up there, the sight below was horrendous. Kwame had landed face down, thus shattering his head. There were splashes of blood here and there and bits of his brain scattered about. He was motionless. His family above wailed.

"Call the ambulance, someone!" cried a man among the residents who had gathered around the body.

Attracted by the sudden wailing inside the flat, the two policemen smashed the door and came in.

"No! No! Please, don't! Let's see what's going on here." said the senior policeman to Kwame's children who tried to escape.

When the policeman looked out of the window, they could not believe what they saw down below. As some of the sympathisers were looking up at the window from below, the police understood that someone had jumped out of the window and not made it.

"It's them! It's the police. They caused this! Look, they are in Kwame's flat!" one fifteen years old Black boy was saying.

The two policemen scrambled down to the scene. Before they got there, some onlookers started accusing them.

"It's you again! It's the police! When will you ever understand that the Blackman is here to stay? I am Black but also British."

It was then that the policemen explained they had come in good faith. They had got a tip off from someone who called from the Housing Estate that a flat in that block, in the one directly opposite Kwame's, was being burgled. When they knocked at the flat in question and received on reply, they knocked at Kwame's own to find out if the occupants knew anything about the alleged burglary or had seen or heard anything suspicious. That was all. And by the way, they were not immigration police. They were simply local policemen on the beat. Even so, the damage had been done and Kwame Kwesi was no more.

****

Immigration police were known for their brutality and ruthlessness. They could cause extensive damage to property and persons in their bid to track down an illegal immigrant. Once they went to a flat to arrest a man from Nigeria and he put up so strong a resistance that they bound his feet and hands, put plastic tape over his mouth and placed a hood over his head. By the time they got to the airport, the man had died of suffocation and so they found themselves saddled with a corpse rather than an illegal immigrant.

****

These were the many thoughts and memories that flooded Martha's mind as she travelled by underground from Finsbury Park to Euston on the first day of her cleaning job. To get to work by 5 o'clock, most cleaners had to get up at about 3 o'clock in the morning, get ready and leave the house at about 4 o'clock. Such movement was particularly taxing in the cold and snowing winter morning. Anyone who travelled by underground or by night bus at those hours, would not fail noticing that most passengers were black young women and men, but mostly women, many of them so tired that they were sleeping. These were, of course, the famous African early morning office cleaners. That was the job a girl like Martha, armed with a BSc in Environmental Management and an MSc in Environmental Waste Management, found herself doing. And how much did she earn from it! Yet, she had no choice because she had bills to pay, rents to take care of, her personal needs to cater for, and of course, her education. She had decided to do a course in computing in the hope that if the tides turned, she could take a job within an environmental NGO. But she wondered whether she would cope, considering the additional pressures coming from home. Incidentally, when that morning's letter from her mother arrived, Martha had just returned from her cleaning job and was resting. Her plans were that once she got up, she would iron her boyfriend's clothes and then go to college for her computer lessons.

****

One of the things that angered her most was that despite her intimacy with her mother whom she felt understood her more than her father, and despite her having told her mother that the cleaning job was no job at as such, she still insisted that she earned a lot of money. Her mother once asked her how someone like her with degrees, could say she was so badly underpaid. Martha painstakingly explained things to her. One, with the economic crisis that had hit her country, the government was no longer sponsoring students overseas. So, she was left in the middle of nowhere. Secondly, although she had two degrees, she could never raise her head in Britain to look for a "proper" job because if the authorities realized her stay had expired, she would be deported. The cleaning job was, therefore, her only option. For those companies that employed people like Martha to clean their offices, this was the cheapest form of labour they could find. Yet, the employees could not ask for their rights because they knew that being illegal immigrants, they had no leg to stand on. So, they put up with the nonsense. The bosses who gave them these jobs knew their status but turned a blind eye to it. But if, as it sometimes happened immigration police turned up, the employers would claim they had no idea their employees were illegal. Of course, the latter would immediately be terminated. But the sackings hardly posed a problem for the company because the very following day, other desperate seekers would be available.

Once in a while an office cleaner helped herself to some of the facilities available, such as the telephone. Some employees made quick calls to friends and relatives within London. Others went further and called British towns other than London. The very bold ones dared to call their families back in Africa. But once the company noticed this abuse, they were immediately sacked. However, for the big international companies, a few brief international phone calls were really not noticeable. And so cleaners lucky enough to work in the big companies, found that the phone was at their disposal when they needed it.

****

Exactly one week after Martha moved into Valerie's flat and three days after she started her cleaning job, Valerie asked her to leave.

"I told you when you packed in without notice last week. So, don't start acting as if you didn't know." Valerie asked her to pack out by 6.00 pm that day. The time was 8.30 am. Martha knew it was pointless to put up an argument with her cousin. What was important for her was to find a place where she would go from that evening.

After Valerie spoke to her, she went into her bedroom and came out shortly afterwards, smelling of perfume and holding her handbag and car keys.

"I'm going to work. Please, make sure you are out of here by 6.00 pm. And by the way, let me have your key of the flat. I hope you haven't copied it."

52

"But Valerie, how will I get in to collect my things? Please..."

"Okay, keep it for now. Once your things are out at the door, lock it and throw the key in through the mail flap."

Martha burst into tears.

"Valerie, how can you treat me like this? You are my own sister."

"I don't know about being your sister. We are cousins as far as I know. At least, that's what my parents say. It's a relationship that I honestly can't explain. And by the way, if you think I am unfeeling after putting up with you like this for up to a week in a difficult large city like London, then you don't know what you are talking about."

"No, Valerie! I am grateful. It's just that..."

"Anyway, I'm late for work. I've told you what to do with the key."

Upon those words, Valerie left and slammed the door behind her.

Left behind, lost, Martha knew she had to miss out on her lessons that morning. After all, what was the point of computer lessons if at the end of the day she did not have a roof over her head?

It was moments like these that made Martha wonder whether she should not return to Cameroon. But then, she realised she had a lot at stake. If, for instance, she left London without regularising her situation so that she could come back in future when she wanted, then she would be burning the bridges behind her. Here where she was in London, opportunities were unlimited, in terms of studies and work. If only she could be patient enough until her stay was regularised, she would win in the end. Why not? After all, others such as her cousin Valerie had made it. Now that such lucky people had become permanent residents and some of them even British citizens, they could come and go at will. That was Martha's dream.

Another problem with returning home was that job opportunities were very limited, in fact, zero. This was because as a result of the economic crunch, her home government had put a freeze on recruitment. The private sector, too, had been squeezed tight by the crisis. So, if she returned top Cameroon, she would simply join the thousands of frustrated graduate job seekers. That was why she knew that despite the difficulties in Britain, that country was her best bet.

****

Martha looked through her address book and copied out some names and telephone numbers. Then she took out some money and went out to a public telephone booth. She called some friends and relatives.

While she made the calls, she reflected on what had just happened between her and her cousin. But being a girl of a good Christian upbringing, she concluded that she would be a fool to take offence at Valerie. After all, in a costly city like London, giving her room, and board was no small help. Having lived in London for years, she herself knew that the great social pressures of the city had forced even sister to chase junior sister out of her flat, for daughter to throw visiting mother out. The list was endless.

After telephoning so many Cameroonians and each of them giving some excuse or other for being unable to take her in (even for a few nights), Martha decided to telephone her university, ate from Ghana, Perpetua, Perpetua was one old friend she had always felt comfortable with, perhaps because they from two very compatible astrological signs. Perpetua being cancer and her friend Scorpio. Occasionally Perpetua took Martha to her church, the Elim Pentecostal Church in the south of London.

The Elim Church was one of the so-called Black Churches in Britain. These were African Churches created by Africans from Nigeria and Ghana. Elim was Ghanaian, like Perpetua. The idea was that the mainstream churches had failed Africans. They were too rigidly "white" and did not recognise that the demographic landscape of the country had

54

evolved and now had an African population that could not be ignored. African Christians had specific problems that needed to be acknowledged and prayed for. These included poverty, discrimination and immigration. In fact, these were problems high on the list of the African community. Unfortunately, the predominantly white churches such as the Anglican, Catholic, Methodist and others, behaved as if these problems did not exist among the black members of the church. That was why the Black Churches were created. In fact, the award winning Nigerian writer, Ben Okri, a longstanding Londoner, did a series of insight articles on the Black Churches in the leading London-published African international magazine, *West Africa*.

****

When Martha mentioned her problem to Perpetua over the telephone, her friend's reaction was prompt.

"No problem. Come and see my flat. I can give you my other room, if you like it."

"If I like it, Peps? But do I have a choice? I'm so desperate that I would accept to pack into anything that looks like a room, even a stable."

"Oh, come on Martha! You won't be a second Christ!"

When Martha got to the flat, she found it to be too good to be true. At twenty pounds a month, she could not ask for better, even though it meant she alone was paying two thirds of the rent with Perpetua only chipping in the remaining ten pounds. She was grateful that Perpetua had been truthful enough to explain to her the monetary mechanics behind it all.

When Valerie returned from work that evening, she was shocked that, one: her cousin had dropped the key where she had asked her to drop it, and two: her things were no longer in the flat that meant she was really and truly gone. She found a note left by Martha on the little glass centre table. It was terse and straight to the point.

55

"Dear Cousin, Val, I have found a place. God has been kind to me. So have you. A million thanks for everything. Stay blessed, Martha."

Valerie sat down and read the note again. She noticed her cousin had left no forwarding address, neither dad she left a contact number. Anyway, she could understand about the absence of a telephone number. Perhaps there was none where Martha had moved in. But why did she not at least mention the London district or borough where she had gone? Valerie herself was in on of the Westminster City Council flats, in central London. So, where could Martha have moved? Hammersmith and Fulham? Brent? Camden? Islington? Dageham and Barking? Tower Hamlets?

For once, Valerie felt remorseful at the way she had treated her cousin. The more the day, weeks, and months came and went, the greater her desire to see Martha again, or at least hear from her. But Martha was in no hurry to reveal herself or her new home.

One day, a year later, they ran into each other at an all-night Cameroonian gala at the famous Africa hall on Ashwin Street at Dalston Junction.

Martha first spotted Valerie some distance away on the dance floor and pretended she had not seen her. But when Valerie saw Martha, she immediately left the man she was dancing with, ran to Martha and hugged her several times while exclaiming: "Oh my God, Martha, how you look good!"

"You, too, Val!"

For some seconds, they stayed in each other's arms. Anyone who had known what went on between them up to this point must have realised that now, there were no longer hard feelings in either person.

When there was a pause in the dancing, Martha pulled her cousin by the hand, "Come, and let me introduce you to my friend, Perpetua. Perpetua, this is my cousin, Valerie. She is also my big sister. She held my hand and showed me around when I first came to London. Valerie, this is my friend,

Perpetua. She is from Ghana and is letting a room in her flat in Finsbury Park."

"Oh! Nice to meet you, Perpetua. Thank you for being so kind to my cousin."

"That's okay. What Martha didn't say was that we were classmates and friends in the university. When she phoned me to say because of the situation in the country, your country, she was having problems with accommodation, having a spare room in my flat, I said to myself: 'what are friends for?'"

"Oh! How nice of you! Here's my card. I live in my house in Westhamstead. Feel free to visit me any time, any day with Martha." She also gave a card to Martha although neither Martha nor Perpetua had any card to give her in return. But it did not matter to any of them. However, Martha wrote out the number of the telephone she shared with Perpetua and gave Valerie. Thereafter, the two cousins stayed in touch with each other.

****

Another year later, Perpetua's boyfriend won the American lottery and they both moved to the United States. They went to Dallas, Texas, to be more precise. Herbert, a Ghanaian like Perpetua, got a job as an engineer in an electronic s company. That was similar to what he commuted to Colchester to do when he was in London. Perpetua happily accepted a teaching job in a university in Dallas, while pursuing her doctoral studies. The best piece of news for Martha was that before leaving, Perpetua transferred her flat to her. Although Perpetua was still the owner, there was no denying that life had smiled at Martha a way it had not done before.

Some months later, Martha met an extraordinary Cameroonian young man at yet another all-night gala at the Ashwin Street, Dalston Junction location. His name was Benjamin Mofor, a medical doctor who was in his second year of specialisation as a paediatrician. He was from Awing village in Santa Sub Division, like Baligham village from which Martha came.

Benjamin had sighted Martha as she sat by herself in the dance hall, while almost everyone else was on the floor. Benjamin happened to be looking for a lady to dance with. Promptly, Martha got up and took his waiting arm. After some summary self-introduction, he remarked, laughing contentedly.

"Benjamin Mofor from Awing and Martha Galabe from Baligham. Isn't that a lovely match?"

Martha smiled but said nothing.

"Are you from the royal family of Baligham? The name, Galabe, tells me something."

"No, not directly. But we are related."

"But that is one and the same thing. If a meeting of the royal family of Baligham were to be called, wouldn't you attend?"

"Of course, I would."

"Yes, Martha. I knew you were only being modest."

As they danced, unknown to them, some single ladies who had been secretly eyeing Benjamin got jittery, because they felt he had slipped through their fingers. They were not acting in concertation. No, far from it, these were some two or three girls, each looking for a breakthrough for herself. It is even doubtful if they knew each other's interest in this golden boy. Nonetheless, it must be said that the idea of young ladies going out of their way to woo young men was a common one at Cameroonian parties. Who could blame them? Life in London was very hard and cash to pay bills was very difficult to come by. Husbands, or at the very worst, boyfriends were equally difficult to get. For that reason, the girls had realised that it was not enough to stay and wait, no matter how attractive one was. It was better to go on the offensive.

Anyhow, here on this night at Ashwin Street hall, the rather shy and unsuspecting Martha Galabe had stolen the show. And Benjamin who had had no intention of looking for a girl when he set out for the party that night, went home a happy man, having thoroughly enjoyed the party and found a great companion as the icing on the cake.

Thereafter, he and Martha kept in touch regularly. Months later, he left his expensive two bedrooms flat within a privately-owned home and moved in to Martha's flat. Although it made life easier for both of them, Benjamin had a lot of family responsibilities back in Cameroon such as sponsoring junior ones in college. Martha, whose upbringing did not make her one to bother anyone, hardly ever made any demands on Benjamin. He paid the entire rents for the flat, which was already great help. Every week he purchased Martha's travel card, which was valid for the underground and the over ground trains in London up to zone 3, as well as the big red London buses within that zone. He "helped" with gas and electricity. But the bulk was still paid by Martha.

Despite all that help, the fact was that Martha was still an early morning cleaner with a pittance of a salary. So, she was still stressed. Imagine, therefore, how she must have felt when receiving stinkers from her mother. That was not all. Sometimes other members of the family sent her letters that were no less vexing. These included aunts and uncles, some of whom now falsely claimed they had helped to educate her.

****

That was the background against which Martha received the irritating letter from her mother. So, after crying, she got up, ironed Benjamin's clothes, he having gone to hospital. He was specialising at one of London's most famous hospitals, nicknamed The Millennium Hospital, on account of its high rating by users.

After ironing, she managed to get ready and go to college. She could not afford not to go. She knew she could use the fact that she was still in full time education to get her stay extended by the Home Office, the British department handling immigration affairs. Her situation was particularly delicate, since she had clearly overstayed in her host country.

The good news was that a Cameroonian-friendly law firm, Antonys and Co., which was very versed in immigration matters, had assured her that her case was winnable. Benjamin told her so too.

****

That evening, Martha got home before Benjamin, and still without looking at that letter again, she put it aside with the intention of talking to him about it as soon as he returned home. That was what she did.

"How bad is the letter?"

"Very bad, Benjy. Very bad."

"Can I see it?"

"Yes, of course. Here it is."

Benjamin took it and sat down. Then he read it quietly and patiently right to the end.

"What's so bad about the letter?"

"What do you mean?" asked Martha, surprised.

"Martha, did you read it through?"

"No. But..."

"Yes, that's the problem. You should have read it through. But what you did was selective reading."

"There you go again," Martha replied. Even so, she knew that compared with Benjamin she was irritable, nervous and impatient. So, she decided to give him the benefit of the doubt.

"Explain all of that to me, then," she said.

Benjamin read the letter to her, slowly, and she listened without interruption:

> *c/o Presbyterian Church*
> *Baligham*
> *Santa Sub Division.*

> *My dear daughter,*
> *It has been eight months since your father and I last heard from you. Are you fine in terms of health? How is your job? And your course? We*

are struggling with the situation back here at home as you know it. There is a lot of poverty and hardship here. People can hardly find money to cater for their most basic needs. People die simply because they do not have money for consultation and drugs. Your father's pension stopped abruptly three months ago without explanation. He has made countless trips to Yaounde and bribed all kinds of officials imaginable. But to this day he has not received a single franc. Instead he is in debt because he has had to borrow in order to go to Yaounde. Last month on December 31 the Head of State in his end of year address said the economy had started turning around. We are still waiting to see in which way.

We are facing hard times here. Despite the explanation you have given about your difficulties, I still believe you could still do more to help us. Your seven junior ones here also need help. Remember you are the only light in the family now. And by the way, how is it that some of the mates with whom you went to England on scholarship and whose scholarship were terminated like yours are still able to send substantial amounts of money to their parents. The son of my colleague with whom we taught Geography at GHS Biwugne has been doing that, so has the niece of my fellow CWF member, Mrs. Tita.

That makes me conclude that you are deliberately hiding your real earnings from your father and me. You are deliberately neglecting us. You no longer send us money. Your father and I are growing old; both of us are senior citizens. Anything can happen to any of us at anytime. We are feeble and in disarray. Only God is keeping us afloat. I don't know how we even cope from day to day. Please, my daughter, send us money. That is what we need. Money for drugs, money for food, money for your junior ones' school needs.

May the good God guide you.

Your mother,
Solange Galabe.

When Benjamin had finished reading, Martha asked him:
"Is that what you call an alright letter?"
"Listen, Martha. The key message in this letter is that your parents need money. I will help you to send some to

them I suggest that you again explain your difficult situation to them. You may be surprised at how well they take it."

With the help of her boyfriend, Martha sent her parents the sum of fifty pounds. That was the largest amount she had ever sent home since the government left them in the middle of the ocean.

Within a month her mother had sent her a most appreciative letter in which she said Martha's father and herself were sending her blessings for greater prosperity. The money proved to be of immense help, especially for people like her parents who now lived in the village where life is not as hard as in town.

Up to this point, Martha had not informed her parents about her boyfriend. She knew they would be hostile to the idea. They called it fornication that ran contrary to the Christian principles they espoused so strongly. A girl should remain chaste until she finds the one she will get married to. And even so, sex should start only after they have become husband and wife, not before.

Martha's parents did not seem to know that rightly or wrongly, things had changed. They did not know that in a tough world like London, it was customary for girls, even those from Christian families to have a boyfriend to support them with their basic daily needs. Girlfriends in turn treated boyfriends like husbands: cooking for them and serving them; washing their clothes and ironing them. And so, life went on. It was either that or the girl perished.

****

One day, Martha's lawyer rang her excitedly.

"Martha, you have won the battle! The Home Office has granted Yours truly, a permanent stay! You can now work in this country! You can get a proper job!"

Martha rang Benjamin, Valerie, Perpetua in America then some other friends and relatives. Everyone pretended to be happy for her, although she knew they were not all genuinely happy.

Within months Martha got a job with an international Non Governmental Organisation (NGO) whose mission was to clean up maritime areas of the world. She was recruited as a project officer at the headquarters based in London. The salary was good.

Alone, she was able to place her parents on a monthly stipend of one hundred pounds. To the parents, this was like winning the lottery.

One day, her parents got a letter from her saying she had found the man of her dreams and they were planning to get married. She went on to say in the letter.

"I know what you are thinking. You are thinking that it is a Whiteman. But it's not. It's someone from neighbouring Awing. He is called Benjamin Mofor. His parents work in Ebolowa, his father as a provincial delegate and his mother as a GHS English Language teacher. He is called Mr. Cuthbert Mofor and his wife Mrs. Bridget Mofor."

"But Ida, I know Cuthbert very well. We were mates in secondary school." Martha's father said to his wife.

I also know Bridget. We were mates at the Ecole Normale Superieure .She was reading English Modern letters while I was reading Geography."

They both rejoiced. Their children hearing them singing, dancing and praising the Lord, wondered what was going on.

"Your sister in London is getting married to someone whose father we know very well and approve of."

"Papa, is she getting married to a Cameroonian, then?" said one of the boys.

Yes, my son. To a young man right here in Awing! God is great!"

Martha's parents wrote back at once to express their profound joy at the news. This time it was her father who wrote. He also started contacting Benjamin's parents.

Back in London, Martha and her fiancé, for that was what Benjamin was now, had not yet picked a date for the wedding. They had not even decided whether it would be in England or back home in Cameroon. in any case, there was no rush. None whatsoever. They were now both permanent residents in Britain. Within a couple of years, they could apply for British citizenship if they wanted to.

One day when Martha and Benjamin both attended a Cameroon community event at the Cameroon High Commission at Holland Park in London, they were surprised at the large number of compatriots who already knew of Martha's new residential status and the fact that they were going to get married to each other. Congratulations! Congratulations! Well done, Benjamin! I'm so happy with you, Martha!" came the chorus.

"Thank you! Thank you so much!" they were both saying.

Martha's joy at the turned tides was without bounds. She was so happy she did not know whether to laugh or cry.

Here at last was the happy ending to the sad tale of her life in London. However, not all in that situation ended up by being successful. In fact, most did not. Even as she rejoiced, she was conscious of the many who where still in hiding, forced into exploitation by unscrupulous employers and harassed by hardhearted immigration officers.

"How I wish this government here would show that in addition to this ancient kingdom and colonial master being a developed country, it is also a nation with a human face, and not a monster hungry for the blood of poor and desperate Africans," she mused.

5

Up in the Air

They had planned it for months. So when they met secretly that Saturday night, it was to do the final touches, the fine-tuning. They were a group of four, calling themselves, 'The bad gang'. Whenever any of them felt like coding their group name, they used "T.B.G.". In fact, they addressed each other by those initials, in order to have a feeling of solidarity while remaining unidentified by outsiders.

Adamu Fon, alias Adam, aged 26 was the gang leader. In his absence, Pius Akwabi, Alias Akwa, 24, deputed him. Solomon Mangoba, 24, alias Sly was the most adept of all. He carried out all the delicate and painstaking jobs. Abraham Nkwenti, alias Docta, was the intellectual of the group. Whereas the other three were primary school leavers, he had reached form five, written the G.C.E. 'O' Levels and passed in two subjects: English and French. When they were in action in a French-speaking town, he was always trusted to communicate in French. At other times, he was the group's secretary, taking down minutes during meetings and read them at the next meeting.

The leader, Adamu Fon, chaired that night's meeting. He was also the host of the meeting, since it was holding at his three bed roomed house in the popular district of the town, Ngubanang.

The gang had been working together for three years. They had met each other by chance at the motor park where usually, young men like them went to look for odd jobs such as finding passengers for commercial vehicles and being paid a token per passenger. Sometimes, they helped with loading goods on the roof of vehicles about to travel to other towns. They also helped to offload those that had just come into the park. It was through frequent contact at the park that they got to know each other. They ate together at the famous makeshift park restaurants. They drank beer together at the off licence when they could afford it.

One fine afternoon, while they were resting in the park after loading up to five vehicles, the group leader, Adam, bought everyone a beer and in the course of their conversation, he said: "Gentlemen, I have been doing some thinking. The work we do here at the park is okay, but I don't think the little income I get from it can sustain me. I can't speak for you people, but although we are not married and have no children under our charge, I still feel I need an alternative source of income. What do you think?"

"I agree with you, boss. But what can we do?"

"The point is, there is a lot on offer around us. It's just for us to define our parameters. If it's money we want, we can get it. If it's goods, there are lots of them about," Adam replied.

"I hope you are not asking us to rob people," Sly enquired.

'Rob? I wouldn't call it that. It's a question of being realistic!"

"How?" Akwa came in.

"Listen boys! We must decide whether we are men or boys. If we are men, then we must know a man's got to do what a man's got to do."

There was silence, as if everyone had decided to reflect awhile. Then Docta spoke.

Let us think carefully. It's true that times are hard. But we must consider things carefully. Stealing or robbery or call it what you like is risky. So, if we want to go into such an activity, we must prepare ourselves well, because if we are caught, things can become nasty. We may find that we need guns to protect ourselves".

"Guns!" exclaimed Sly. "But I don't want to kill anybody."

"No, nobody is asking you to kill anybody. If we carry guns, it's simply for self-defence. Do you mean that if someone shoots at you, you will not shoot back?"

Sly said nothing. Then there was a minute of total silence, after which the leader ordered another round of drinks for everyone.

By the time they dispersed, they had reached a consensus that they would "use those alternative means" to increase their income. They agreed that there were a lot of opportunities in the town and that all they needed was guns. There were, for instance, shops with goods and their daily takings to offer. There were banks. There were fairly wealthy private homes. However, they also agreed it would be too premature to venture into the "big deals" just yet. So, nobody should think anything about breaking into a home or a shop yet. For the next few months, they would be finding out, discreetly, as much as possible about the trade, so to speak. While doing so, they agreed that individually or in pairs, they could start practising pick pocketing at the park while performing their duties as park boys. They learned through experience that the best moment to pick pocket was went passengers were alighting after just travelled into town or when they just arrived at the park and were being contested by different park boys. Another opportunity was when people crowded round an herbalist explaining the efficiency of his products.

One day when a woman in a hurry arrived at the motor park and park boys rushed to her, one seizing her suitcase, and another her sack of corn and the third her three year old daughter, Adam who was obviously more concerned about implementing the agreement agreed by the gang, flung himself at the woman: "Why are you people troubling this woman? Leave her alone! She will choose which vehicle to travel in by herself."

Within those few minutes and unknown to the passenger, Adam had successfully opened her handbag, removed her purse and pocketed it. No one saw him do it.

The woman only realized her purse was missing when she got to her destination and was looking for money to pay for the journey. She wept bitterly.

"Oh, my purse, oh! My purse is gone! They stole it!"

Moved by her predicament, the driver let her go. But he did so without in the least knowing that at the end of the day his master would deduct the fare from his monthly wages.

"I employed you to do business not charity," he said to the driver callously.

In a way the theft of the woman's purse was as a result of negligence on the part of the ticket salesman at the Mokunda motor park Normally, passengers bought their tickets at the starting point before boarding the vehicle. But when she got to the park, she was immediately rushed into a waiting bus incidentally labelled "God's time is the best". When she asked about the ticket, the driver dismissively said:

"Don't worry about it. You will pay when we get to Ngogbong". And so she settled down comfortably. The ticket salesman actually saw from his tiny office, the woman climbing into the bus and settling down, but neither said nor did anything about it.

But again, one can never be too sure about these things. Sometimes drivers connived with ticket vendors in this way and they later split the unrecorded fare among themselves. At other times, when the driver was sure the ticket man had not noticed anything, he proceeded with the passenger and pocketed the entire fare.

When Adam counted his booty, it amounted to thirty thousand francs, which was a lot. That was twice his monthly wages for working as a park boy. When he revealed the amount to his three acolytes, they felt encouraged enough to be able to affirm that they would beat Adam's record. And they set about it in all earnest. Later, Adam gave each of than FCFA5,000 and kept FCFA15,000 for himself. They were all happy.

But unknown to them, by robbing the poor passenger of FCFA30,000, they caused distress to an entire family. The woman had travelled to Mokunda to collect that money from her son, a businessman, in order to address some emergencies that had arisen in the family.

Her 5 years old son was ill and she needed FCFA11,000 to purchase the drugs the doctor prescribed. Another son, aged 13 had been sent home from the college for non-payment of tuition fee. He was doing building construction at a good private college of technical education in the town. He needed a minimum of FCFA10,000 to return to college. In addition, there were other household needs to take of. Her husband was on retirement, a senior citizen as they were popular called. So, there was no way of relying on his meagre pension that was already irregular, anyway. As might be expected, the loss of the money caused untold misery to the family. Bur did the gang of four know that? Did they care? Once one becomes a criminal, does one not become callous, cold-blooded, unfeeling and a killer?

Fired by the determination to beat their leader's record, the other three members worked tooth and nail. One day, Akwa ran into a golden opportunity. He had just finished unloading a vehicle when he noticed that at the other far end of the motor park, a crowd was gathered. He wondered what might be going on, but decided that whatever it was, it could still go there and see if he could "make some gains" on unsuspecting onlookers. So, he rushed towards the crowd and once he got close to them, he leaned against some of the people, saying in pidgin: "Na weti di happen for here! Na weti di happen for here?"

While he did that he quickly searched the pockets of victims and removed their money, wallets and purse, and quickly stuffed them into the several pockets of his jacket. He made the sum of FCFA9,000 in cash, two wallets with a total of FCFA16,000 and one purse with no money in it. He was verifying these things in the public pay in toilet at the park. When he had finished, he put the wallets and purses in a plastic board that he then dropped in the dustbin and hurried away.

Sly went about things in his own way, as usual. Instead of looking for victims at the motor park, he decided to go to the main market that was nearby. His aim was to seek out a wealthy traveller who was shopping prior to boarding one of the long distance buses. He found one, a man in his mid fifties, trying on a suit in a ready-made clothes shop.

What drew attention to the men was the fact that he overheard him telling the shop attendant that he was hurrying to catch the next bus for Bulang town. He was going to be best man at a wedding. Sly went out of the market and waited for him at the exit into the motor park. As soon as he saw the man struggling with a large plastic bag in which his new suit was, two suitcases and his brief case, he immediately moved into action.

"Bulang town, one more seat! One more seat for Bulang town! Anyone going there?"

"Yes, please, I am going to Bulang town."

"You are lucky. Let's go," said Sly, trying to get some of the man's luggage.

He let Sly take the plastic bag and his brief case.

"Hurry or you'll miss the bus! That would be a terrible thing because you would have to wait for the next one which may take hours to fill up before departure."

"No! No! No! Keep that seat for me!"

"In that case, let me hurry ahead of you and ask them to hold it."

Sly then quickened his pace and within a couple of minutes he was already out of sight, separated from the traveller by people going in all directions, busy doing their own things. As might be expected, when the traveller got to the vehicle, he could not find his "helper" or his luggage.

"Where is he? Where is he?" he asked trembling.

"Where is who, sir?" asked a busy park boy.

"The man who gave me a hand with my luggage. I was just coming out of the market. He said he was coming to reserve a seat for me."

"What is his name, sir?"

The traveller looked stupid. He had not bothered to find out the name of the young man. So, there was no one who could help him with the problem.

Abandoned to himself, he wept like a little child.

"He has gone away with my luggage. That suit is very expensive. What will I wear at the wedding? And my briefcase!" he said weeping even more loudly as if his very life depended on that suitcase.

"The suitcase contains my important documents such as my National Identity Card. It even has all the money I have left..."

But no one was really listening to him seriously. A small crowd had gathered around him. But this was more for entertainment than for help.

"What misfortune is this? What misfortune have got into?" he said as he left the park on foot. Sly, meanwhile had boarded a taxi for his home, his one bed roomed rented property at Meta Quarter, where he pushed the plastic bag containing the suit under his bed. He placed the suitcase on his bed, forced open it and marvelled at its contents.

Later in the evening when he recounted his exploits to his colleagues, they all congratulated him for a job well done.

****

Abraham Nkwenti, alias 'Docta'. After looking at a number of options. Decided to try a supermarket owner. He knew him because often, the man personally drove members of his family to the motor park to catch a bus. Docta knew that the man was very receptive and generally received people who called at the supermarket to see him. He was also fond of leaving his guests in the office in order to go the toilet or solve some shop problem or another.

When Docta entered his office 'Busy man' was just finishing a telephone conversation.

"Sit down, young man. What can I do for you?"

"I came. I came to see you for assistance, Sir. We who work at the motor park want to make better use of our lives. We need assistance to buy some books we can read when we have no customer and are bored. We..."

The telephone rang and after answering it by just saying: "Okay! Okay! Fine, I will do, I will do." He got up and said to Docta: "Just a minute, please." Then he went out of the office and shut the door behind him.

Quickly, Docta looked around to ensure nobody was watching him. Satisfied, he moved swiftly to the businessman's seat and pulled the top right hand drawer. In it he found at least ten bunches of five thousand franc notes, seven bunches of ten thousand franc notes and eight bundles of two thousand franc notes. He quickly removed one bundle of ten and two of five. Then he shut the drawer and quickly went back to his own seat. He was lucky because as soon as he sat down, the door opened and there was Busyman.

"Sorry, I kept you waiting."

"No problem, sir."

"Yes, you were saying…"

"Please, sir, I would like to get to President of the reading group. He can explain it better."

"Where? Where is he?"

"He is down stairs. I mean, down stairs. He is outside," he stammered.

"Outside" Why outside?"

"He is discussing with his uncle … He … He met him when we where about to come up to your office."

"Anyway, call him up."

Docta left. Half an hour later, he had not returned, neither had his so-called President. As Busyman waited, he carried on with his work. He pressed the button of his table bell and his secretary, Alice, came in promptly.

"Can I have the Credit Union File."

"Yes, Sir."

Throughout that day, Busyman waited in vain for Docta. He, however, did not notice that money was missing until the following day when he opened the drawer to contribute to a young people's fundraising event.

"Bloody hell!" he exclaimed as he rummaged through the drawer, thinking that some of the bank notes were hidden in the corner or in some of the envelopes and old letters that were in it.

"For sure, the money is gone, Alice." He screamed forgetting the bell.

"Has anybody entered my office in my absence?"

"No, Sir. But remember you left that young man of yesterday in your office alone for some time."

"You're right, Alice," he said, pursing his lips and clenching his fists. "Yes, I wish I could strangle him!"

"What is the problem, Sir?"

"He stole my money! He removed money from my drawer! That bastard! I wish I could kill him!"

All this while, the two young men who had come to seek a donation sat opposite him, helpless but praying that he would still be able to give them something in support of their cause. When he had sat down he opened the drawer, removed ten thousand francs and gave the boys.

"I am sorry. If this had not happened I would have given you twenty or even thirty thousand francs. But, alas."

As the boys thanked him and were leaving, they heard him ask his secretary what was the name of the "thief".

"I don't know, Sir. I didn't talk with him, Sir. But I believe he wrote it on the audience request form which is with you."

At that point the two visitors left the office and as they walked downstairs, they lost track of the conversation between the boss and secretary. However, the conversation went on.

"I can't find the form." The boss was saying to himself. "It's not on my table where I put it. That criminal must have taken it away. He's a criminal of the first grade."

What Busyman did not know was that as soon as he left Docta in his office and he leapt to his feet before opening the draw, the boy picked up the form, crumple it into a tiny ball, put it in his mouth, chewed it and swallowed it. The idea was that if the businessman came back in, looked for it in vain and happened to ask him about it, he would swear he knew nothing about it; and if he had to be searched, nothing incriminating would be found on his person. For one week, Busyman mourned the loss of his twenty thousand francs. He talked about it to anybody who came into his office, or those he came across outside of his office. Thereafter, the theft became less and less of an issue until he stopped talking about it altogether.

****

This was how for over a year, the four boys were never caught. That emboldened them to carry out many more attempts.

Nonetheless, that Saturday night they met for final touches, it was about what one would call 'the mother of all robberies'. The Bad Gang, or 'TBG' as they called each other, was getting ready to rob a bank in the town called "Starboard Bank International". Starboard was the local branch of a European bank.

They, but especially Gang Leader, Adam, had taken the pains to get to know the two night watchmen of the bank and had even made them friends. The idea was to ensure that if on the night of the robbery any of the night watchmen were away from work, the other would still be able to help them. They told them that if they co-operated and made the robbery successful, they would earn a lot of money.

"You will have enough money for you and your families to live comfortably for many years to come," Adam told them.

"In fact, you will find yourselves earning up to a hundred times your salary," added Akwa.

Pa Ngong was already making mental calculations of what exactly a hundred times his salary represented. It was forty-five thousand francs multiplied by a hundred. He remembered what his teacher, Mr. John Buteh Ndiangang had taught them in primary school.

"To multiply by a hundred, simply add two zero's to the figure your are multiplying."

In Pa Ngong's case, this meant four million five hundred thousand francs.

"Massa!" he thought, "with that kind of money the future is safe."

Pa Memba also accepted the proposal because he needed the money. He was going to build himself a decent home and use the rest of the money to buy a taxi that he would recruit Apollo, his nephew, to run.

****

The plan was adequately discussed and rehearsed by the gang and the two night watchmen. They would wait for one of those nights when the bank manager worked late to launch their assault. Occasionally, Mr. Boniface Nsawir, did come to the bank at about 9 p; until 11 pm. Since it was not possible to know in advance when he would come to the bank, it was agreed that the four would be alert so that once they saw the lights in his office were lit, they would know he was in.

One day when it was Docta's turn to check the bank manager's office lights, he found that the lights were on. So he hurried back and in less than an hour the four were at the bank. That was according to their well-rehearsed plan.

Adam led the gang. When they got there, they found Pa Ngong on duty at the entrance.

"Are you alone?" whispered Adam.

"Have you come" No, I'm not alone. Memba is inside with the boss."

"Okay, we need to get Memba out before we get in."

As Docta stood there, a wave of fear ran down his spine. For some reason he felt frightened at what might happen, and that was despite all the 'training' he had received for over a year. However, he managed to pull himself together.

"Man die, ye die," he said, making the sign of the cross.

Sly was a short distance from the rest, "inspecting" the premises. He was looking for escape routes once the task was completed. Akwa was standing close to the gang leader and listening while he talked with the night watchman.

"Let me go and get Memba out," said Pa Ngong as he tiptoed away.

When he got to the locked window of the boss, he coughed three times. That was his little signal with his colleague. But to the bank manager, that was just Ngong, as he called him, coughing.

"I want for go piss, Sah," Memba said, making for the door. The manager gave him a nod of approval. He noticed that this was the first time a night watchman had asked for permission and without waiting for a reply, had already started executing. At any rate, he thought nothing about it any more

As soon as Memba stepped out, the three members and Pa Ngong rushed to him: "What' he doing?"

"He is counting bundles of money and putting them in a safe."

Quickly, the gang leader got out some ropes from a bag Docta was carrying.

"Quickly, tie up the night watchmen, Akwa. You, Sly, take this portion of chicken blood and throw it on them."

A few minutes later, the manager's door flung open. He was about to put some more bank notes in the safe. Unfortunately, he was caught in the act. So, frightened and still in his seat with the bank notes in his hands, he managed to say:

"Who are you people? What do you want?"

All three bandits pointed guns at him.

"Stand up and raise your hands! Thundered Adam

He complied.

"If you do as we say, you won't be harmed. But don't try any tricks, otherwise we'll shoot you. We'll kill you. Come on, take these two bags and fill them up!" he said, throwing the bags at him.

"Come on! We don't have time to waste!"

The manager was so frightened he could not call any of the night watchmen. The guns were pointing at him as he filled the bags. When they were full, Adam said:

"Bring them here and lie on the floor, face down. Go on, then! Or do you want to die?"

"No! No! I'm doing what you asked."

Grabbing both bags, Adam turned round and called out to his mates:

"Let's go, guys!"

Unknown to the robbers, the bank had a secret security link with the Gendarmerie Brigade. The device was fitted such that whenever thieves broke in it would go off and alert them into action. Unfortunately, on that night, when they got the signal, they could not act at once because all their patrol vehicles were out. When they got to the bank, the manager was pacing up and down in his office and screaming:

"The bastards! The bastards! They even got my night watchmen!"

When the Gendarmes asked the night watchmen which way the robbers had gone, they both pointed to the wrong direction.

Just then, a second vehicle with three gendarmes. Bringing the total number to seven, arrived and the commanding officer issued instructions.

"Major Achidi, take four men and go in that direction. Major Efouba, you and the others come with me!" Both vehicles gave chase. They drove quickly because with their sirens activated, they could drive through red lights.

It was the Commandant's group that soon spotted a yellow cab trying to force its way into a narrow side street. Seeing the Gendarmerie pickup coming behind, the taxi driver quickly reversed into the main road and carried on ahead. The Commandant felt these must be the robbers they were looking for. And it was.

What happened was that the gang at gunpoint stopped the first taxi they saw when they left the bank.

"Take us quickly to Brimonga quarter. Do so, otherwise I will shoot you."

"No! No! I beg you. I will take you to anywhere you want to go. Just don't kill me! I have a family ..."

"Shut up and drive!"

"Yes, Sah."

****

As the Gendarmerie pickup drew closer and closer, the gang started panicking.

"Accelerate! Accelerate!" Adam shouted.

"He is doing his best, boss."

"You shut up, Akwa! Since when did you know about driving?"

The poor driver increased his speed and as he negotiated a bend, one of the back doors suddenly flew open. As he attempted to balance the vehicle, one of the bags slipped out of Adam's grip.

'Wait, you fool! Can't you see my bag has fallen out?

"I can't stop, Sir. The Gendarmes are behind."

When the Gendarmes got to that point, because, thanks to their headlamps they had seen the object drop from the taxi, they stopped. It took them about three minutes to find out because it was dark and they manipulated the headlamps. They found the bag and picked it up. They were later to find that it contained eleven million francs.

Back in the taxi, Adam and Akwa were quarrelling because the latter felt that since Adam had already lost one bag, he might lose the other. So he should give it to him.

"No, I won't!" backed Adam. "I will keep it. I am the leader of this group."

"But you have already lost one!"

"And so what?"

Thereupon, Akwa grabbed the bag and a tug of war ensured. In the process, the rope that tied the top of the bag came off and bank notes flew all over the place; some inside the vehicle, others outside and going up in the air. The top speed of the car helped in making the notes fly faster.

"You see what you have done?" said Adam, raining blows on Akwa. Sly and Docta tried in vain to separate them. While they fought, they let go of the bag.

78

As the driver negotiated another bend, both the front door and the same back door that opened before, flew open and the bag with whatever was left in it went out. The Gendarmes saw this.

The fighting clearly impeded the driver's manoeuvres, so he slowed down. At that point the Gendarmerie vehicle quickly overtook them and blocked the way.

Seeing what was happening, Docta got out and attempted to run.

"Stop or I shoot!" challenged a gendarme pointing a gun at him. The gendarmes were professional armed robbery fighters, while the gang was made up of amateur robbers. They could not be any match for the gendarmes. Within minutes, the gendarmes had arrested the four TGB's. They also took the taxi driver with them but later released him on the grounds that he was simply a victim of circumstances. The matter went to court and a couple of months later, the gang of four was jailed. Adam got four years; Akwa, three; and Sly and Docta two. The night watchmen got six months.

6

The coffin maker

He had been thinking about it for some time now. In fact, ever since he noticed the demand for "proper" coffins in the town had risen, he began toying with the idea of branching off into the manufacture of coffins. He envisaged a situation in which instead of doing what other carpenters did, that is, making coffins and selling them as and when the need arose, he could now make them in advance and in anticipation and display them in the front shop permanently. In that way, anyone who needed a coffin could simply walk in and choose one. What was more, he could make them, ensuring that the prices were different, depending on the sophisticated nature of the coffin. As time went on, the idea of manufacturing coffins became more and more settled in the mind of Thompson Asongwed.

His current workshop was located in one of the town centre quarters of Kana town, the provincial headquarters of on of the country's ten provinces. The workshop, which bore an overhead board saying, "Asongwed Modern Carpentry Workshop: come here for all your needs." was perched at the angle between Ngaruwah Street and Bangoji Road, a strategic point which had one of the largest number of drinking spots in the town.

Thompson opened the workshop some four years ago, with financial assistance from his uncle - a junior brother to his mother. Andrew Akotoh, for that was his name, was a medium businessman in the town. He had a large store in Kana town where he sold essentially building materials. In addition, he ran two heavy-duty trucks - one a 20 ton and the other a 12 ton - which plied the route between Kana and Ngongntum, the national economic capital. Basically, the trucks travelled to Ngongntum to transport goods destined for the uncle's shop. But prior to setting out for economic capital, Akotoh and close collaborators had to find another businessman or organisation or firm in possession of goods to be transported to Ngongntum but with no lorry of their own. In this way the proprietor of the trucks ensured that none of the truck's journeys was wasted.

Long before Thompson opened his carpentry workshop, he used to assist in his uncle's business. He had dropped out of secondary school at the end of Form One, having been dismissed for failing his promotion examination. His uncle who sponsored him, his father having died tragically in a road car crash, got so angry that he said he would not spend a single franc again on him. So, going back to school for the poor boy was out of the question.

However, soon there was a change of heart on the part of Thompson's uncle, the reason being that he realised the boy had acumen for activities that had to do with practical know-how. The boy was good at making things with his hands. He made paper kites and flew them; he made paper planes and ships. He even made wooden bicycles.

When he left school, his uncle got him to help out in the store. So, he helped in selling and moving the stock around. He helped in loading goods bound for Nongntum and offloading goods just arrived. Sometimes he accompanied one of the truck drivers on the journey to the economic capital – a long trip, he realised.

One day Thompson's uncle sent for him.

"Do you still make those things I saw you making with wood?"

Thompson, a boy of fourteen, suddenly went numb. He froze like a five year old caught in wrongdoing.

"No, come on! Don't be frightened my son." his uncle said taking him by the hand.

"Do you still carve those your things? The wooden bicycle I saw you riding, for example?"

"Yes, papa."

"Thompson."

"Yes, papa."

"It seems you are very good at handiwork, and especially wood work. I have arranged for you to develop that skill. Today is Friday. From Monday you will start an apprenticeship with Paul Tado, my friend who owns the carpentry workshop on Fon's Street. Do you know him?"

"Yes, papa."

"Okay. So on Monday report to him at 7.30."

That was how the young Thompson started his training as a carpenter.

****

That was some years ago. Today Thompson was not only his own master, but he actually had apprentices working under him. Although he thought of heading "Asongwed Modern Carpentry Workshop into coffin manufacturing, he also felt it would be disastrous to do a complete u-turn away from the supply of goods other than coffins. So he simply decided to scale them down while laying emphasis on the coffins.

As he thought things over, more and more people died - or at least he had that impression. As a result, his resolve about the coffins became stronger and stronger.

It must be recalled that this was the period in the life of his country, Manam, when the dreaded HIV Aids pandemic was wreaking havoc. Young men died, young women died and the older grieved about parents having to bury their children instead of the other way round. "What has this life come to!" they wondered aloud.

What finally made him take the bull by the horns was the fact that by 4.00 pm on a certain Thursday - if the name of the day matters - he received up to three orders for coffins; one for a 16 year old college student, one for a 24 year old married woman, and the third for a 37 year old civil servant. Needless to say, they all died of Aids. Those were more orders he could handle, especially as they were urgent.

The following day, he called his workmen and told them: "From now on we shall make sure there are at least ten ready made coffins on standby in the shop. That will save us the trouble of losing orders or being put under pressure. Besides, it will guarantee that income comes in regularly."

There was no room for questions and since it was not a debate either, that brief meeting ended there. Before the boys went home on that day, Thompson got them to prepare some heaps of plank and plywood so that the next morning work on the coffins would start.

****

The next day, they started work early and went straight to make the first coffin. Wood was sawn and planed by about midday. By 2 pm they had finished putting together the various bits and pieces. By 4 pm, they were already polishing it.

As they worked outside in the front yard of the workshop, passersby noticed they were making a coffin. However, they did not show any disapproval. After all, was it not just a coffin? Someone must have died somewhere as they did so often, anyway.

That was so good so far, but trouble began a few days later when Thompson felt that with four coffins made, it was time for some publicity. So he had the coffins displayed on makeshift tables in the yard in front of the shop. A notice on a signboard pointing towards the building from the road said: "Choose your own coffin here."

It did not take long before passersby started stopping as they walked past on the road to see if they were not dreaming.

"Coffins being displayed to the world so blatantly? What has this life come to?" one man asked. Shortly afterwards the number of standing passersby grew. It became a crowd. They discussed excitedly.

"I have lived in this town for 15 years, but never before have I seen anything like this." Passing taxi drivers stopped their cars to ask what was going on. Private vehicle owners swelled the ranks. Then a businessman, known popularly as 'King of Youths' drove by. "What is going on here?" he asked. There was a chorus of responses too discordant for him to make any sense out of them.

"Please, speak one at a time. I can't understand."

Speaking directly to one man in the crowd, King of Youths said: "Anton, you tell me. I know you can speak well."

"See for yourself, Sah. Look at what our town has been reduced to."

So far, Thompson's boys had noticed the curious crowd but did not let it bother them. So, they continued working away at the next coffin, the fifth. This was inside the workshop, out of view of the crowd.

Nonetheless, as Anton spoke to King of Youths, pointing to the workshop, two of Thompson's boys bore out the fifth coffin they had just finished, and were going to display it alongside the other in the yard.

"You see what I mean?" shouted Anton to King of Youths. Then angry shouts came from the crowd: "Remove those coffins or we'll break them up."

"Keep quiet! Keep quiet!" King of Youths was trying to calm them down.

"No! No! Why should we be quiet?" questioned one of them.

"A coffin shop? Have you ever heard of anything like that? A coffin shop? Even Paul Tado has not opened a coffin shop!"

"Wait! Hold on. What is the problem?" King of Youths asked thoughtfully.

"The problem is that we don't want any coffin shops here. Are they praying people should die so that they can make money by selling their coffins?"

All this while, Thompson's boys installed the coffin they had brought out, stood and looked at the crowd for a few minutes and went back into the shop.

But once they went in, someone on the road shouted: "Look, they have gone to bring out yet another coffin. Shall

84

we just stand here and watch them frighten the town to death with their coffins?"

The man who just spoke was Anton. As soon as he finished speaking, he turned to the others and said: "Let's go." Not even King of Youths could stop them. They fell on the displayed coffins and broke them up. When Thompson's boys came out to stop them, the assailants who were about twenty and up to five times the number of Thompson's apprentices, beat them up and actually left one of them bleeding through the nose.

In that disorder, King of Youths drove to the Gendarmerie Brigade and within an hour, three Gendarmes were at the scene. Unfortunately, by the time they got there, some the attackers had run off. They arrested four men whom they took to the Gendarmerie Brigade. They also took Thompson's men.

When they asked Thompson's boys who was the boss of the workshop they gave the Gendarmes his details. However, since he was out and away at the time of the incident, the Gendarmes said he must also report to the Gendarmerie Brigade. King of Youths was not there. In fact, once he alerted the Gendarmes, he went his way, not wanting to be found out as the one who blew the whistle on the attackers. It appears it was really never known that he was the one who did it. As a result, he never got any reprisal from the "gang" so to speak.

****

When Thompson arrived at the Gendarmerie Brigade, and went to the Gendarme on duty, his first words to Thompson when he heard his name were:

"Ah! C'est vous le fabricant des cerceuils?"

"What do you mean?" asked Thompson pretending that he did not understand French, the official language of the country.

"I dong talk say, na you dong make cerceuils?" the Gendarme said in pidgin which was understood by many people.

"Yes, I make coffins."

Thereafter, the Gendarme spoke to him in pidgin. He told Thompson that the Brigade Commandant would receive him in person. Meanwhile, he was moved to an adjoining room and made to sit on a bench with other people apparently waiting to be received by the Brigade Commander. But he was given no explanation.

"Ah! Ah! Thomson!"

"Good morning, Uncle." It was a former colleague of his father's.

"What brings you here, my son?"

"Well, They haven't told me yet, they say it's the Brigade Commander I have to see. But I believe4 it is in connection with an attack at my workshop, by some young men in the town."

"What happened, my son? You mean they attacked you?"

"No, I was out. But they attacked my boys and destroyed my goods."

"What did they destroy, son?"

"Coffins."

"Coffins, my son? How many?"

"Five!"

"Five? What were you doing with five coffins? You mean you received an order for five coffins?"

"No, Uncle. I made them just in case."

Thompson's "Uncle" whose name was Akuma, but he was popularly known as "Pa Akuma," then went quiet and reflected for some seconds.

"I can understand you, my son. A lot of people are dying and the need for ready-made coffins is real. However, you must understand that readymade coffins are not yet part of our culture. It will, therefore, be some time before our people come to term with that. You must therefore be patient."

Just then, The Commandant's secretary picked up the phone that had rung and said: "A vos orders!"

She was dressed in the Gendarmerie uniform and wore two v-shaped stripes, therefore a Gendarme-Major. Her name badge read: Alice Nguena.

"Mr. Thompson Asongwed!" she announced, pointing to the door leading to the Commandant's office. Thompson got up and entered the commandant's office.

As soon as he opened the door, the Commandant who had been writing, stopped writing and raised his head.

"Asseyez-vous, s'il vous plait."

Thompson sat down, the commandant watching him closely. Thompson noticed the office was very tidy - unusually tidy. The desk did not have much in terms of paper work, just a few books, some files, and a penholder with a number of pens. Basically, that was it. Thompson noticed the nameplate that was colourful and beautiful.

"Mdl Chef Arouna Bello, Commandant de Brigade."

The 'Mdl' he knew, was in French and stood for "Marechal des Logis," although he was in English. Anyway, he decided that was not very important because the Gendarmes were not part of the English cultural heritage to which he belonged.

Learning backwards in his seat, the Commandant broke the silence,

"Que s'est-il passe chez vous?"

"Sorry I don't understand French."

At that point, the Commandant switched to English. "No problem. I will speak English. I was a Gendarme Major in Kumba for eight years you know?" He smiled.

Thompson did not return the smile. So putting on a more serious air, Arouna asked: "What happened at your place?"

"Well, I wasn't there..."

"Yes I know you were out."

"Yes. Some boys came and destroyed my goods and beat my workmen."

"Why did they do that?"

"Well, I can't tell."

"Quel dommage. You say they destroyed your goods. What goods were they?"

"Coffins."

"Coffins? Coffins? You make coffins?"

"Yes, I'm a carpenter!"

"I know you are. But how many coffins did you have in your shop? How many did they destroy?"

"There were five displayed in front of the shop and they destroyed all five."

"You mean you made five coffins and put them in front of your shop?"

"Yes"

"Why? Did you already have five dead people?"

"No, we made them just in case?"

"Is there any another carpenter in this town who does that?"

"I don't know... I don't think so. I don't know of any."

"Anyway, Mr. Asongwed. What I will do now is ask you to formally give us a statement. I will send you to one of my men. You will have to make a written statement and sign it. Or better still, you make your statement to him, he types it and you sign."

The Commandant paused and gave Thompson an imposing look. Thompson looked up and became psychologically intimidated.

"Okay chef," he said to the commandant.

The commandant sat up in his swivel seat; swing it around, giving the impression that he was looking on the short side table that stretched along showing off his chair.

Almost immediately, he swung back to his table and placing his hand on table bell button, he rang. Almost immediately, the lady secretary appeared: "Call ne Nguessi."

"A vos ordres!" she replied, standing at attention.

Seconds later she left the room closed the door behind her. A minute later, Nguessi knocked and came in; the commandant addressed him in French.

"I want you to take a statement from Mr. Asongwed about the incident that took place at his workshop. Alright?"

"A vos ordres, mon commandant."

Nguessi said, saluting firmly. After that he opened the door and the commandant gestured to Thompson to follow him.

****

The exercise lasted for about half an hour with Thompson sitting on a wooden chair with a backrest separated from a poorly made but crowded table at which Nguessi was working.

Nguessi was using a typewriter that Thompson noticed was old and rusty. Some of the characters had come off and the buttons had been replaced with little tablets of wood improvised for that purpose. The original missing letters, he noticed, had then been hand written on the make shift objects. Looking around, Thompson noticed that apart from the machine he Gendarme Major was using, the only other one visible at the Brigade was that of the female secretary who had announced him to the Brigade Commandant. What intrigued the carpenter most, though, was the fact that although Nguessi used only two fingers to type he was quite fast. When he finished typing and read through, he pulled out the sheet from the machine and gave it to Thompson. After reading it, the later told him: "It's correct, chef."

"Sign, then." Nguessi replied, Thompson signed, after which the Gendarme told him he could leave but would be contacted if necessary.

"But if there is any further trouble from those boys, come back and tell us."

Thompson got up, pulled in his seat under the wooden table on which they had been working. Then, he searched in his pocket, got out a FCFA2,000 note and gave the Gendarme, saying: "Chef, this is for your drink."

"Thank you Patron. Thank you very much." Nguessi replied getting up and smiling from ear to ear. The truth was

89

that Nguessi had not seen a FCFA2,000 note for over a week. It was the 25th of the month of August, precisely the part of the month referred to as "twenty hungry" because money from the previous month's salary was finished, yet the next month's salary was not actually due until a week or so later. This was a situation that applied to all civil servants, not only Nguessi. Anyway, the comparatively few gendarme officers who worked on the highways and other streets were better off because they were able to extort little bribes from taxi and other vehicle drivers "caught" in one offence or another. But alas!

Thompson shook hands with Nguessi and left.

****

As soon as Thompson returned to the workshop, his boys told him that some men had been there and warned them not to make any more coffins.

"What was it they didn't like about the coffins?"

"They said making so many coffins at a time is not good because it means we are praying for people to die quicker and earlier so that we make money."

"But that's not true, Pius and you know it."

"It's not so, Sah. That's what they said."

"Sah, they also said if they see any more coffins in the yard, they will burn down the shop," added Ezekiel.

"Were these the same people who broke up the coffins in the yard?"

"No, sah. They were different."

"Do you know any of them? Had you seen them before?"

"No, Sah. Never." responded Pius, the most forthright of the apprentices.

"Anyway," the boss said after reflecting for a minute, "the Gendarmerie wants us to report any more attacks or even threats. So if it happens again, that is if they come back, let me know."

He re-iterated that message when one of the boys suggested that if they continued to be "persecuted" thcy drop coffin manufacturing - or perhaps scale it down and step up the making of other usual items such as furniture.

Anyway, they took their time with the coffins. By the time the week ended,- that is within five days - they had this time made only one as opposed to three previously. At the same time they produced kitchen stools that were very much in demand at the time and some beds. This cautious approach was partly dictated by the fact that although there had not been any more threats, the workshop nevertheless was visited by people whom, it was clear, could really not afford to buy the articles they were asking about, or were not willing to buy. That led to Thompson and his team concluding that such people were agents or spies for those who had vowed that a coffin shop would not be allowed to stand in Kana town. In other words, it must be killed; the reason being that it's very existence represented a death wish on the part of those who owned the shop and made the coffins. Therefore, instead of waiting for the coffins to kill, it was necessary to kill the coffins first.

As another two weeks ended, Thompson now felt that since they already had four coffins made and the fifth was near completion, when that fifth was finished, why not once more display them outside in the yard? After all, no new threats had been executed yet. Besides, the Gendarmerie was on his side. Once in a while, one or two Gendarmes would pop in to ask if all was well. It did not seem to matter that he had to tip them by giving them what they called "money for fuel" before they came to the shop and also give them their "drink" at the time they were leaving the shop.

Two days later, and buoyed by the early afternoon sunshine that shone on Kana town like some immortal torch from above, Thompson had the five coffins displayed in the yard. However, little did they know how much trouble awaited them, as you, the reader, will soon come to know.

The news of this second attempt at exhibiting coffins so "blatantly and stubbornly" to quote the Principal of the largest mission college in the town, (even him) spread like wild fire and within half an hour, the premises of the workshop was assailed and the workmen, including the boss, Thompson, assaulted. Old men, young ones, old women and young girls stormed into the compound, some carrying cutlasses, some clubs, others axes, and all fell upon the coffins in frenzy.

Thompson tried in vain to stop them, so did his boys. But it didn't work. After smashing the coffins to pieces, someone poured petrol on the bits and pieces which had been gathered into a heap, and set it all ablaze.

"This is money! This is my money going like this!"

Thompson protested trying to wrench himself from those who were raining blows on him. It was not so much himself he was interested in. It was the coffins, because he reasoned that if he sold all five, he would make around two million and five hundred thousand francs. But he was that money going up into flames.

As if that was not enough, someone shouted: "Bring that petrol can let's also burn down the workshop."

Another said: "That's right. In that way, we can be sure he won't start again. He will give us peace of mind."

Minutes later, the workshop, too, was in ablaze, Unable to free himself from the "enemies" who held him back, Thompson threw himself on the ground and sobbed. His boys, who had attempted to put up a fight, had given up. But they, too, were being kept in check. So, there was not much they could do, apart from watch as their careers and that of their boss were being reduced to ashes.

"Oh my God! What have...What have I... done to deserve this?"

Thompson wailed.

"What have you done? You have blasphemed against the very God you are calling. A man dies before you make his coffin. You don't make it before he dies. If you do, you are pushing him to death prematurely." said one of the attackers.

Another proclaimed:

"If you think you can open a coffin manufacturing industry in this town, you are wasting your time because it will never work. We're not a doomed town. If you want to be a death merchant, go somewhere else. We can't accept you here."

Just then, a car - a private one - pulled up on the main road and the man driving it came out, looked in the direction of Thompson's shop and exclaimed:

"What! What is going on here?"

"We have burned down the evil that was taking root here." said a bystander.

"What evil? What are you talking about?" enquired the man who parked the car, as he went nearer.

"Are you a new man in Jerusalem? Don't you know the man who owned this workshop, that fool they call Thomas, was running a coffin shop here?"

"Yes, and that's why I have come. I was told at the General Hospital that if I came here I would be able to choose and buy a ready-made coffin on the state. Do you mean the coffins have been burned down?"

"It's not me saying. See for yourself. You can see the place has been razed to the ground and all that remains is smoke and rubble."

"Oh no! What shall I do now? I need a decent coffin for my father who is lying in the General Hospital mortuary."

"You will have to go elsewhere."

"But where? How about the wasted time?"

"Wasted time? Is that all that bothers you? How could you want to buy a ready-made coffin? Don't you see it is ill luck? Did the manufacturer know your father was going to die? Can't you see this can lead to other deaths in your family?"

"I don't understand your manner of reasoning. Are you saying ready made things that are bought lead to death?"

"No, not all. These are coffins we are talking about, man! A coffin means death. The manufacturer is calling death by showing it these coffins especially when they are openly and blatantly exhibited in the yard, as was the case here. By the way, are you a new comer to Kana town?"

"No, I'm an old man here. I am a businessman in this town. I have been a builder here for twenty years. We have watched Kana town grow from scratch and even contributed to its development."

"But then, have you ever seen such a thing happening here before? A carpenter pre-empting death by making coffins in advance and boasting about them?"

"No, not in this town. But I have seen it somewhere else."

"Well, Kana is Kana and not anywhere else."

Unknown to the businessman, Zik, his interlocutor was a philosophy teacher. In response to the unknown philosophy teacher, he sighed, turned round, entered his car and left.

By this time, the crowd had grown smaller as people realised that the climax was over and left either one at a time or in twos or threes. Even those who "held captive" Thompson and his faithful men had released them and left. Thompson and the others, aided by some sympathisers, were trying to put out the fire. Even so, it was too little too late. There was nothing more that could be saved. Curiously or mysteriously, only the signboard, "Asongwed Modern Carpentry Workshop," could still be seen dangling in the wind. The second part of it: "Come here for all your needs" had been burned off. So were parts of the words above: "modern" and "workshop".

It was at this point that the Gendarmes came to the scene. It was the commandant himself, accompanied by a Gendarme Major - another one, not Nguessi.

"Thompson! What happened? I've just been informed. Why didn't you call me?"

"This is it, Chef. This is what I've been reduced to: ashes. It has just happened."

"Quel dommage! Did you insure your shop, the equipment or the goods?"

"N, I didn't. I didn't think it was necessary."

"Oh la la. Quel dommage!"

****

As they spoke they were joined by King of Youths who also claimed he had just heard about what happened. Although he was not one who held any top public position as such in the town, his opinion nevertheless, counted. So, Thompson was pleased that King of Youths had come.

"What happened, my son...? Oh Commandant? Are you here, too."

"I am here, King of Youths. We were told about this."

"Is it the same group of people responsible, Mon Commandant?"

"Well, that's not how we look at it. At least, we can't tell at this stage. We'll pick up this incident as if it was a fresh one and work on it. If it has any leads to the past, we'll of course follow them up."

"You made some arrests after the last incident here, Mon Commandant?"

"Yes, those men are still being held by us. One of these days we'll transfer them to "awaiting trial.""

Turning to Thompson, King of Youths said: "What happened this time, my son?"

"They came again, King. They came back. They have burned my entire workshop."

"Sorry, Thompson," King of Youths said as he contemplated the rubble, ash and smoke.

"They burned everything. If it were only the coffins, I wouldn't mind too much, because I could always make some more. But look, my planks, some planed, others crude, are all gone. My tools are gone and my expensive woodwork machine, bought by my father... They're all gone. Reduced to ashes."

At that point, someone cried out: "The Mayor's coming. Look, that's his car pulling up!"

95

Everyone looked up at the main road and there was the mayor, Paul Munya, popularly known as the Lord Mayor stepping out of his service Toyota pick- up double cabin.

The three men went up to the road to greet him. The Commandant gave him the military salute, and then shook hands with him. Next came King of Youths with another handshake.

"We were together, King, two hours ago, yet you told me nothing about this?"

"Did I know, Lord Mayor? I didn't. I had no idea. I've just learned about it."

"So have I," enjoined the Commandant as if to excuse himself, although he was not required to give details of information to do with his job to the Lord Mayor.

"Are you the owner of the shop?" the mayor asked, pointing to Thompson who was still standing with King of Youths and the Commandant.

"It's me, Lord Mayor."

"I hear you exhibited coffins here?"

"Well, we sold coffins."

"But I'm told you made many and exhibited in your yard.

"Yes, that was to make people know we had them."

"I understand. But that is scary. I'm sure that's why some people took offence."

"But that's no reason for anyone to commit the crime of arson, Lord Mayor." the Commandant snapped in.

"I didn't say so, Commandant. But we must ensure there is peace in the town. I'm sure you're conscious of that, Commandant."

"Of course, Lord Mayor."

****

Sometimes, Thompson felt sorry for himself and wondered whether someone had not cast a spell on him. Had he known, he would say, he would not have ventured into this coffin business at all. These thoughts bothered him a lot, especially when he was in bed at night and could not sleep.

To make matters worse for him, he was single, which meant there was no one for him to share these unsettling moments with. Had he a wife, she could have placed a hand on his shoulder and said something like:

"Don't worry. God knows best."

Unfortunately, here he was, left to his own devices and at grips with reconciling the questionable goodness of a God who was neither seen nor heard and a stronger force which made him descend further and further into the abyss of destruction.

As the weeks elapsed, he found that he had become notorious in Kana town. Often, people came up to him and asked why he wanted to bring ill luck to the town.

"Me?" he would ask, surprised.

"Yes, you."

"In what way?"

"By doing everything to wake up the dead."

"What do you mean?"

"You are piling up coffins, yet there are no deaths yet. So you are doing everything possible to push us into our coffins prematurely."

Another person would say to him:

"I know you are a carpenter. But why don't you make something else? You can make furniture, for example."

"But we need coffins," Thompson would argue

"Aha! That is the problem. Who needs a coffin? You? You standing here? So have you made one for yourself already? Or are you interested in making them only for others? Have you made yours?"

"No... I have... I haven't..."

"Well, you see, that is what I mean. In any case, I am only trying to advise you."

There were times when Thompson would walk along the street and find people talking to each other and pointing at him accusingly. It also happened that he would go into a drinking place and no one would want to talk to him. Once he asked for a drink and the man serving asked him mockingly.

"Do you want your beer in a glass or a coffin?"

Everyone in the off licence burst out laughing. Unable to take it anymore, Thompson got up. However, as he was about to leave, the bartender said: "You haven't paid for the drink."

"But I haven't drunk it. I haven't even touched it."

"But it's been opened."

"I know it's been opened. I didn't ask you to open it."

"But you didn't ask me not to open it."

Just then, another man who was drinking and chatting with a woman nearby, snapped: "Pay for the drink, you coffin maker!"

Suddenly, blood rushed to Thompson's head and his heart beat faster. He stood there, mad with anger. He clenched his fist, made a move towards the man and then stopped.

As if stung, the man who was old enough to be Thompson's father got up and challenged him.

"You want to fight me? Come on, then."

The man's companion, the woman, pulled him gently by the hand.

"No! No! Pa. Don't do it. Let the man go!"

The man retreated and sat back down. Thompson dropped his hand, felt in his pocket, paid for the drink and left.

****

One night as he lay in bed, his father appeared to him in a dream. They were both in the coffee farm that stretched all around in the compound. They were harvesting ripe coffee as they always did at that time of the year. They were at nearby coffee trees, each of them pregnant with ripe coffee fruits. Father and son had a basket each in front of them. Each time they had a handful of ripe coffee, they would throw it in the basket.

"Tom!"

"Papa."

"How is your business doing?"

"It's not good, Papa. My workshop has been burned down."

"That is exactly what I want to talk to you about."

"I'm listening, Papa."

"Tom, you need to be cleansed. There are evil spirits around you. Ask your father, Andrew to take you to someone who can fix you up. You must protect yourself from those evil spirit."

Just then, Thompson woke up and found he was in bed. Yet, what had just happened looked so real. He felt that if his late father told him was workable, then he could very well continue with the coffin business.

The truth is that despite all the hostility, no one really took the carpenter aside to ask him what he thought about the business. Yet, in his heart of hearts, he felt very strongly that there was need for such a business in Kana town. He did not believe it was right for anyone to wait to have a corpse before having a coffin made.

Despite the recommendation Thompson's father made, there was not much he could do - at least for the time being - because his uncle Andrew Akotoh was out of town. In fact, he was out of the country, having gone to one of the neighbouring countries to prospect for business. Having heard that there was a good market for Irish potatoes in Koula Republic, he decided to experiment with a small quantity of the community. If it worked, he would move into that line of business.

As soon as Andrew Akotoh returned from Koula, he sent for Thompson. He sent his driver, Pius and his Pajero Jeep Paratrooper with the instructions:

"Go and fetch Thompson for me."

Although we say he sent for his nephew "As soon as" he r3eturned, let us not exaggerate the emergency because this was the day after he returned from Koula. In fact, he got to

Kana town - with the same driver, the same driver of the Pajero - in the late hours of the night. Worn out by the journey, he was received by his wife, Martha, and children. He had a bath, ate something and then retired into the eager hands of his wife who had dearly missed her husband for days.

When Thompson got to his uncle's house at Ntongo Quarter, Andrew Akotoh had just finished breakfast and was up against the sitting room mirror, adjusting his tie.

His did not hear his nephew come in.

"Good afternoon, Papa."

"Aha! Good afternoon, my son. My driver found you?" he asked, motioning to him to sit down. Thompson sat on the four-sitter sofa that formed a square along with the single three-sitter and three single sitters that made up the set of seats in the sitting room. His uncle sat two chairs away from him, on the single sitter that he had specially decorated the traditional way. Andrew Akotoh was a notable in the village. He was a "Ntumfon," which means 'the Fon's Ambassador' or 'envoy'. That was title given by a Fon, and once one Fon gave it to any worthy man, the title was recognised by any other Fon anywhere. However, apart from the nobility status, Akotoh was a descendant of the royal family; so was Thompson's mother, his sister. In fact, his name, 'Akotoh' was that of a previous Fon of the village, the grandfather of a current monarch.

Nonetheless, as far as Thompson was concerned, what he was thinking of at that moment was his late mother whom he was seeing as he sat there with her brother in a photograph on the wall opposite where he was sitting, just above the television set. It was a photograph his uncle had taken with his mother, their two other sisters and one brother - all of them now deceased, apart from Thompson's uncle, Andrew. What stroke Thompson here was the marked resemblance his uncle and mother bore with their own mother.

"Thompson!" said he, while placing the case of his reading glasses on the centre table which was surrounded by the set of sitting room seats

"Papa."

"I hear you've been having problems at the shop while I was away?"

"Yes, Papa."

"What happened?"

"The workshop was burned down."

"How? By whom?"

"I have been accused of making coffins."

"Why? What do people say about it?"

"They say I am inviting death prematurely."

"So, who burned the workshop?"

"Some people from the town. It was more or less mob action. I can't really tell you who did it."

"Have you informed the authorities?"

"Yes, they were there, the Brigade Commandant, the mayor, the Special Branch Police Commissioner and even King of Youths."

"Do you want to continue in that line of business? I ask because there is also the option of carrying on with carpentry but limiting it to the manufacture of other equipment, leaving out coffins. How about that?"

"The coffin business is good, Papa. It gives ready cash because once a man has lost someone and can get an immediate coffin without waiting for it to be made, that is very good news."

"Okay. How badly burned is the workshop."

"Completely burnt. It's completely burnt."

"What does your landlord say about rebuilding the place?"

"He says I must rebuild it myself if I want to keep my business there. And if I want to move out I must still rebuild it because it was a built structure when I moved in."

"Have you made an estimate of what it would cost to rebuild and re-equip the workshop."

"Yes, Papa. It's three million francs."

"Fine. I'll give you half of that amount as a personal contribution that is non-refundable. But the other half must be refunded so that I can also help your brothers and sisters who are still at school. Out of the one million and five hundred thousands can you pay eighty thousand francs a month until you pay off completely?"

Oh, thank you, Papa. But since I'll have to start from scratch, can I pay fifty thousand francs a month?"

"No problem, my son."

Thompson did not tell his uncle about the dream. Unknown to him, he was to pay the price later. A week later, reconstruction work began at the site of the burned down workshop. But this time, Thompson and his uncle took a number of steps: the recommendation: "come here for all your needs," was left out of the notice board which simply read: "Asongwed Modern Carpentry Workshop." Coffins would no longer be publicly displayed out in the yard. They would be made and locked up in a storeroom next door. When buyers came and enquired, they would then be shown in. Thirdly, Thompson's uncle "greased the palms" of the Gendarmes and Police so that they could keep an eye on the shop regularly. One month later, the new look workshop opened its doors with emphasis being laid - as agreed - on alternative goods, not coffins.

The ongoing reconstruction work at the workshop did not go unnoticed by the general public, especially neighbours and passersby. Word quickly went round the town.

"The coffin maker is rebuilding his burnt down workshop!"

It was more or less like the words, "King Midas has ass' ears," that were in one of the English readers used at the time by primary schools in the country. Nonetheless, the commandant's men kept an eye on the place. From time to time one of them would pop in just to ensure everything was fine.

"No problem, Chef, Thompson would say, occasionally adding: "I mean, so far."

As the days and weeks went by, Thompson and his boys continued to make coffins that they carefully kept in the nearby storeroom. Most customers who came in were interested only in the odd coffin. In their grief, they selected the coffin that matched either their sense of aesthetics or their budget. Once they paid for it, they left. Most of them did not seem to be people from Kana town, at least not to Thompson and his workmen. But then again, they could very well have been from the town, for, Kana was not a small town. It boasted some one million souls, had four high schools, four secondary schools, nine primary schools and five nursery schools.

As far as the sale of the other articles such as furniture was concerned, it was no cause for concern. Business was encouraging. Buyers who did not like what they saw on display in the yard could simply move into the workshop hall and look at the next set of goods. The coffins were safely out of view in the storeroom and only accessible to customers who had come to purchase a coffin - and needed one desperately.

However, that calm was soon to change dramatically - yet again, the signal for that being the death of the mother of the mayor of the town, Paul Munyo alias "Lord Mayor."

The Mayor's mother, popularly known as "Big Mammy" died at the Provincial hospital after being hospitalised for exactly seven days. At the start she complained of stomach pains, then had a runny stomach. After that she felt feverish and transpired profusely. As soon as the Mayor was informed, he had her moved to the hospital where she was immediately taken in care by Dr. Charles Ndeh, a physician and surgeon who had trained in Nigeria and Kenya and had long made his mark at the hospital on account of his thoroughness and good results. Dr. Ndeh examined her and started her treatment. Two days later, her symptoms stopped. On the fourth and fifth days, she felt better. The following day, she said she was well and asked the doctor to let her go. The doctor, of course, said no. His reason was that since Big Mammy was advanced in age - 75 years old - even if she felt better, it would not hurt observing her for a few more days. And in any case, this was the Lord mayor's mother, anyway.

On the sixth day, Big Mammy got up earlier than usual, made her bed (for the first time since her admission in the hospital), had her bath, dressed up, and sat on her bed and started singing and praying. Other members of her ward (the female ward or "F" ward) found this rather odd about her. However, it was also felt that she could not really be a member of those new wave African-rooted churches that were characterised by sabre-rattling, high-strung and ostentatious worship and condemnation of everyone else. Nonetheless, they wondered what she meant when she kept exclaiming, looking satisfied with herself, in pidgin:

"My heart dey sweet like honey for inside!"

A man whose wife was on a nearby bed asked Big Mammy: "Why your heart sweet for inside so?"

"Because I dong see God. I fit die me now sef," came her reply.

Even so, the idea of her talking about being able to die now surprised onlookers because she looked cured totally cured. Nonetheless, one of the last things she did on that sixth day of her hospitalisation was to send for her son, the Lord Mayor.

The Mayor was informed at about 6.30 pm, when he was still treating some files in the office. By the time he reached the hospital, it was 8pm. It was past visiting hours, but since this was the Lord Mayor, no questions were asked and no one attempted to stop him. Instead, every hospital employee he came across treated him as if they had spent the whole day knowing he was coming and, therefore, waited for him. So, they literally gave him red carpet treatment. Therefore, it pays to be Lord Mayor.

When the Mayor walked into the ward, he was equally surprised at how well his mother looked.

"Sit down, my son," she said, pointing to the lone metallic chair that stood between her bed, F123 and bed F124, and was, therefore, intended for both patients or their guardians or guests. The mayor sat down, looking at his mother with stupefaction. Curiously, there was some commotion in the ward as other patients, their guardians and even the nurses on duty and the ward servants each tried to steal a glance at the mayor who had done them such an honour by coming right down to them. In a growing town like Kana, anyway, the mayor was one of the biggest persons. In fact, if an important personality - including even the President of the Republic - visited the town, the Mayor would be the first person to read a speech.

However, to the old woman on bed F123, this was not so much the Lord Mayor as it was her son. That was why she pressed the point.

"My son, my heart dey sweet like honey for inside."

"Why do you say that, Mamma?"

"Because God dong talk for me today."

"How did he talk to you, Mamma?"

"God dong talk for me for dream. God dong call me, tell me say come up and stay here with me. God tell me say my husband dey with ye for heaven. God want me for heaven."

"But, Mamma..."

"No... Lefan so. "But" no dey for God palava! Wuna pikin dem ask question too much."

The poor mayor left it at that. Deep inside of him, he did not feel upset. He loved his mother too much too be annoyed with her. If today he was mayor of Kana town, it was because she had virtually single-handedly raised him. His father had lost his job as a truck driver and lived and died with the injuries he sustained because the insurance companies that were supposed to pay him never told the truth. He left Paul's mother and five children with Paul as eldest and lone son. All the girls were married and Paul, naturally his father's successor. So, the mayor changed the topic.

"Mother, have you eaten?"

"Yes," she said, but immediately went on to say, yet again: "My heart dey sweet like honey for inside."

The mayor did not say anything this time. But he turned his chair so that he sat facing his mother sitting on the bed.

"Paul!"

"Mamma." And Paul looked up at his mother. He found that her eyes looked distant, vague, somehow misty, like the type of cloud one sees through the aeroplane window when in flight. It was that type of cloud that made distant places look so close.

"Paul, when I die, bury me for coffin with soft white inside and coated gold inside."

"I will do so, Mamma."

"Now go home and tell your wife, Edith, and the children that I am well. I am coming home soon. I should have left this hospital already. What am I still doing here? It's only that the doctor wants me to stay for a few more days." "Okay, Mamma," he said, getting up.

"And another thing," she said as she stood up as if to see off her son. "Ask Julia to bring me hot pap for morning. I want chop pap for morning."

That night Paul's mother who had now been joined by two of her four daughters was more alive than ever. She sang, prayed, told stories and even gave her daughters useful pieces of information about the history of the family. This happened fir about five hours until 10pm when one of her daughters, Martha, realising that she was looking tired and sleepy, told her: "Mamma, why don't you have some sleep? You must be tired."

However, Martha realized she did not have to say that because her mother, who was already lying in bed and tucked in, was already beginning to snore lightly.

In the middle of the night, groaning from her mother awakened Martha. She shook her.

"Mamma! Mamma! What is it?"

"Nothing, my daughter."

"Then why are you groaning?"

"Oh, well. It is that man. He was putting his foot in the door and stopping me from entering."

"Which man? Which door? Where?"

Then Martha found that her mother was already fast asleep. She, too, went to sleep and thought nothing more of it.

In the morning, this was day 7 of hospitalisation, Paul's wife, Julia, was early with pap. She was the first visitor in the ward, having got there at 6.30am.

As soon as Martha saw Julia walk in, she exclaimed: "Aha! Mamma can have her pap now."

Then she called out to her mother but got no response. Pulling the blanket from her mother's face, she found her eyes shut but her mouth unusually agape. She started trembling and saying: "What is this? What is this? Let it not be that..."

Some powerful current ran through Martha's body thus making her scream very loud: "Oh my God."

But before she could even scream her sister and sister-in-law had already flung themselves at their mother - or rather, what now remained of her - for she was dead.

No amount of touching, turning, tapping or shaking brought any life into Big Mammy. The three women burst into tears. There was general commotion in the ward as everyone sought to find out what was going on. Only patients who could not leave their beds were the exception. Even so, they were all ears and watched closely.

When the nurse on duty got to the scene, she quickly pulled the curtains to screen the bed and asked the three women to step out.

"No! I can't. This is my mother!" said Martha.

Her junior sister who usually did not talk much, did not go out neither did she put up any arguments or justification. She just stayed and was allowed to stay. They were all in tears, all of them, including Julia who said she must leave in order to inform her husband, Paul, the Lord Mayor.

Once Paul got the news, he rushed to the hospital and had his mother's corpse transferred to the hospital's mortuary, as was the case with bereaved people who needed enough time to give their beloved one a befitting burial. If that were not the case, Paul would have started making arrangements at once. But then, he was not an ordinary citizen to bury his dear mother in a hurry or in secret. He was the one and only Lord Mayor of Kana town.

When Paul returned to the office that afternoon, he found people waiting to present their condolences. Some had been to his home and been told he was in his office. Together with some close persons, he wrote an obituary that he quickly sent to the provincial radio station for broadcast on the following day's midday national network programme "News from around the country."

In two days, when Paul started making funeral arrangements for his mother, the big issue of the coffin inevitably came up. He remembered his mother's words: "Paul, if I die bury me for coffin wey i soft and white for inside and i get gold coat for outside."

Before leaving home that morning, he discussed it with his wife - but well away from his children whom he felt were too young to hear a conversation about death and burial. He had a boy aged 9 and two girls aged 7 and 5. His wife remembered vaguely that she had heard of a certain courageous young man who opened a coffin shop in the town

"I know about it, dear. I even know where the shop is. I'm afraid it was burned down."

On the way to the office, he asked his driver, Isaac, whether he knew the shop.

"Yes, Sir, I know it."

"But wasn't it burned down?"

"It was, Sir, but he rebuilt it."

"Oh! You see what this work can do to someone? Something happening in my own town and I don't know about it. Yet, I probably authorised the reconstruction."

At that point, he wondered to himself what happened to those young men who were arrested when the shop was burned down.

"Why don't they just let the poor boy run his life the way he wants? He isn't harming anyone," he thought.

"Isaac! Sir."

"Do they still make coffins in that shop?"

"I don't know, Sir. Before it was burned down, coffins were sold there. They could even be seen displayed in the yard. But today what one sees in the yard is ordinary furniture. So I don't know."

"That's alright."

Once at the office, he was reliably informed that Thompson Asongwed's Carpentry Workshop was back in business and still selling coffins, but discretely. He was advised on how to go about it.

Following the information Paul was given, he sent someone to check discretely whether he could rely on Thompson for the kid of coffin he needed for his mother. The person he sent was he Council's treasurer, Nyako Yusufu. He went with Paul's driver, Isaac. When they came back they confirmed that, one: Asongwed Modern Carpentry Workshop was indeed in business; and two: the type of coffin Paul needed was available. Paul had told them the cost did not matter, as long as it was what his mother wanted. After all, was Big Mammy not the mother of the Kana town Mayor?

A couple of days later, on the Friday the corpse was going to be removed from the mortuary, Paul decided - rather unwisely - that the convoy of vehicles bound for the mortuary, should stop at Thompson's, collect his mother's coffin and then take it to the mortuary. After removal of the corpse had taken place, there would be a church service and later an all night vigil at his home, followed by burial on Saturday morning.

When the convoy got to the workshop, things went out of control quickly because once the Mayor, his treasurer and driver as well as the four Council workers who were supposed to carry the coffin went into Thompson's workshop, other people - in an attempt to be in the town's mayor's good books - tried to be helpful by also following them into the shop. Before the Mayor realised it, up to eight uninvited men had forced their way into the storeroom where the coffins were kept. Not Thompson's boys nor Thompson himself could stop them.

"We are with the Lord Mayor," they said.

And they were led in, because who in K - Town could stand in the way of the Lord Mayor? Even the Senior Divisional Officer had to be careful because many had come and gone, yet that Lord Mayor remained.

Anyway, when the coffin was paid for and taken out, the uninvited men left with the mayor. But surprisingly to Thompson and his employees, the same men returned about half an hour later, brandishing axes, machetes, hammers, sticks and clubs, - and even fists - shouting out angry insults as they rushed into the yard.

"You swine, Thompson! Come out! We know what you do here. You still make those coffins. We saw them. Is it I you want or the coffins?" Thompson asked as he walked out into the yard, calmly.

His boys were behind him, bearing their own weapons, ready to fight back.

"Where are the Gendarmes who are supposed to be guarding this workshop?" he thought to himself, trying to conceal his internal fright.

There were some moments of silence.

"We don't want you. We want to destroy those coffins."

"Then you'll have to destroy me first."

The gang leader, a certain unemployed ex-convict called Sadam Hussen, stepped forward and challenged Thompson:

"If you don't step aside at once we'll either push you aside and pass or we burn the workshop."

"I know you can burn it down because you have done it before..."

110

"No, it wasn't us, but that doesn't stop us from doing so now. If you continue to block us."

"Go on, then!" said Thompson.

Upon a signal from the gang leader, women jumped upon Thompson and held him down. The other men wrestled with the workshop mates while one of the eight-sprinkled petrol he carried in a ten litre plastic drum on to the furniture outside and on the coffins in the storeroom. Once that was done another man lit a match and within minutes, the whole place went up in flames. Thereupon, the assailants turned and fled.

There was a huge crowd now gathered at the scene, some members of it trying in their own way to put out the fire. Unfortunately, petrol fire is very wild. It's not like the ordinary one that consumes village thatched roofs and can easily be put out with water or wet banana leaves, like it happened in Mbalum's compound once.

Surprisingly, Thompson was very brave. Instead, it was his boys who wept about this continuous losses wondering what would now become of their future and that of their families. But above all, what would their master do now?

Thomson's only response to them was: "Come on, boys let's leave this place."

No serious help came because the focus of the town on that Friday was the removal of the Mayor's mother. Event he uniformed men who had been "paid" to guard the workshop had gone. They did so on the pretext that no one in his right thinking senses could stay away from such a big event in the life of the Lord Mayor. But deep in their hearts, they knew that was not the real reason. They went there to enjoy the much cherished free food and beer.

"That one na big die," they said.

When the Lord Mayor learned of the burning, he was in the church service and if he did not disrupt the service out of disgust and revulsion at what he called a diabolic act, it was out of respect for the great woman he was in church to honour: his mother.

"Have they been arrested?" he asked his informant.

In any case, arresting the gang members did not matter to Thompson who had already made up his mind about what action to take. He would attend the Lord mayor's mother's burial the following day, Saturday, spend Sunday seeing the people dear to him, and on Monday, he would leave K-town and settle, probably where there was already a multiple of coffin makers who had been accepted because the town dwellers had got used to the idea. His conviction had not diminished one bit. He just felt that his own people in K-town were not ready for this revolution yet. Or was it, he wondered, that a prophet was really never accepted in his own hometown? So, if he had come from somewhere else to settle and sell coffins, as he wanted, would they then have accepted him? Thompson followed his action plan to the letter. On Monday he left K-town and at the border, shook the dust off his feet.

7

Homecoming

Isidore Wamuvud felt very strongly that he must make the trip to Ongola as soon as possible, in fact in two day's time that meant on Sunday night. The overnight trip (this form of transportation having become very popular because of its practical nature) he felt was the best option. He would travel with one of the Agencies, most probably family crown, for their reliability, so that he could get to the capital by 5,30am. That would give enough time to unpack, have a bath and rest before going to the Ministry.

That Friday night, Wamuvud could not sleep. He kept turning over and over in bed. This night was different from others because that phone call he had been expecting for up to year had come. A man he had been "tipping" since he introduced his retirement benefit payment dossiers in the Ministry of Finance had spoken to him earlier that evening to say the Minister had given his accord for his money to be paid. When the son of the neighbour told him at whose house he received his calls since he, like the overwhelming majority of citizens had no telephone, he missed his step twice before getting there. Even so, it must be said in all fairness to him that he did his best to carry himself, for man of fifty-seven.

Atangana was brief, perhaps because he had waited on the other end of the line for to long.

"Monsieur Wamuvud," he said in French, "I have good news for you. The Honourable Minister of Finance has approved payment of your benefits? So, you must come to Ongola as soon as you can.

For a man who had not had a single franc paid to him since he retired two years ago, this was too good to be true. Wamuvud's heart missed several beats. Thinking he was about to have a heart attack before receiving the good news, he asked Atangana whether he could sit down. But Atangana had already hung up as the line repeated the telephone-down sound. Wamuvud sat down, clutching his weary but excited heart in an attempt to calm it. "Are you okay, Isidore?" inquired his neighbour, Pius Shu, the Chief of service in the provincial delegation of culture at whose house he was taking the call.

"I'm fine Pius. I'm alright," he replied as he tried to steady himself out of the room. When he got to his house, some ten minutes walk away, his wife who suspected the call had to do with the retirement benefits looked at his face only once as he hurried along and knew that it was good news. They both hugged each other and danced for joy.

The noise drew the attention of three of their children who were at home - it was holidays, the long-term holidays after which children who did well in their promotion examinations changed classes. Deborah Fri aged 17 had just written her GCE Advanced Levels and Vitalis Anomah aged 13 had just been promoted to form three. The other children were away, some playing with mates outside, others running errands and yet others spending the holidays in the village with the extended family. "What's the good news, Dad?" Deborah asked, "Oh, Debbie, your father is needed in Ongola to process his documents for retirement."

"Is that why you people are so excited, mum?" said Peter.

"Come on, son, you don't know how long I've been waiting for my dossier to get to this stage. Can you imagine what it is like, for a man, a family man, to spend years without receiving a single franc in income? It is even more painful if you have been a salary-earning worker. If your mother had not been doing petty trading, how could we have survived up to this point? Even so, the market for Irish potatoes has become flooded and so her income has dropped. If your children were not in non fee-paying government schools, I would not have been able to send you to fee-paying schools. I have never been able to understand why it takes so long for civil servants in this bloody country to get paid retirement benefits that are theirs by right" By this time, the children had withdrawn.

"But you know, my dear. You know why. It's because there are selfish and corrupt officials out there who will sit on your dossier until you give them a "tip" before they move it on. It's called bribery and corruption. It's the system. The country is rotten, this country!"

The couple's frustration was understandable, in the three years since Isidore retired from the provincial Delegation of Agriculture where he was Chief of service for statistics, life had been rough, financially, and he had borrowed from here and there to make ends meet. Even so, it was very difficult. For a man who had been robust only three years ago, he had begun to shrink, he had lost weight and aged a bit too quickly,

"Although the going is tough, don't give up, darling. God knows your needs and will provide in the end," his wife would say. And she was better placed to do so. For years she had been hardened by the ups and downs of the trading business in which one spends a lot of time making and losing money and chasing bad debtors who make promises that they break with surprising ease and unconcern. It was hard for her husband who was used to being paid a fairly regular salary every month without having to run after anybody.

It was all of these thoughts that made it difficult for Isidore Wamuvud to sleep on that Friday night.

"Is it the news from Ongola that is making you so restless, my dear?" asked his wife.

"You know it is," he said laughing.

There was one thing that united this couple: their outspoken nature. They always felt free with each other and hardly bore any grudges, whenever there was a problem, they would talk about it and bury the hatchet. They understood each other well. And so Julia knew that as her husband's mind was set on going to the capital in two day's time, nothing could stop him.

"Can you start packing my things early, that, is from tomorrow morning, so that you don't forget any item?"

"Yes, I will. Do you know for how long you will be away?"

"Oh! I can't tell, perhaps a week, you can never tell when it comes to chasing dossiers in that place. First, everyone that you come across will want a tip. Then some will even go as far as sitting on your dossier until they get what want. I don't know where this country is heading. It was not like this before, that is, when we joined the civil service. As you will remember, it has been hell for me pursuing my dossiers through the Ministry of the Public service."

"Have you called your brother, Edward to inform him to expect you on Monday morning?"

"No, not yet. But I will do so first thing in the morning".

The said brother was actually Isidore's cousin who was teaching in one of the Government Bilingual high schools of the capital. Each time Isidore was in the capital, he stayed with him and his family. On Sunday morning, the day Isidore was to leave for Ongola, he was the first to get up. In fact he was up by five o'clock and woke up his wife.

"Julia, Julia, Julia"

"Yes, What is it dear?"

"You know it's today I'm going to the capital?"

"Of course, I do dear"

"Okay, get up and let's pray!"

"Pray? About what?"

"About the mission. I am going on a very important mission. Remember my benefits are expected to amount to around three million francs. Well, lets say one and a half millions, considering that half is used for kickbacks. Those bloodthirsty scoundrels! Why for God's sake is this country so?"

Julia got up and her husband holding her hand said a short but meaningful prayer in which he thanked god for mercies and asked him for blessing as he left for this all-

116

important mission. He also requested protection for his family, "if anything happened to him."

"If anything happens to you, why did you say that? Why should anything happen to you?" asked Julia, looking surprised.

"Well, dear, you can never tell. You know man proposes but God disposes."

As Isidore's wife packed his things later that afternoon, he came into the bedroom and asked her if she had included the wedding photograph.

"The wedding photograph? What for? You want me to remove it from the wall and put it in your briefcase? Why? And what will replace it in that space?"

"Yes dear, let me take along, the space can be empty for now. After all, I'll be away for only a week. And what does it matter if I am away for longer? The Photograph will be returned...And by the way, can you include a photograph of yours and those of the children?"

"Each of the children?"

"Yes, each of them, but you may simply include the group family picture."

Isidore left the bedroom but returned later to say he also wanted his wedding suit to be packed with his things. At this point, Julia decided that it was pointless to show surprise or ask any questions. But secretly, she wondered whether this was one of those occasions when her husband felt he must affirm his man-ness over the woman. Or was the money he was about to get already making him behave irrationally?

The night he was about to leave home, Isidore got his family together and they prayed. Then he asked his son, Peter, to carry his suitcase and see him off at the Family Crown Agency. But before he left, he kissed each of the other children and then his wife to whom he whispered.

"Julia, take care of the children."

"I will, dear. You know I will."

When he took his seat on the bus and it was about to leave, he looked out at Peter below from his window seat.

"Son, take care of your brothers, sisters and mother"

"I will, dad."

They waved to each other as the bus took off and drove out of the Agency. The ambulant salesman got up in the bus and started rattling to passengers about the wonder drug that could cure thirteen different illnesses. Some passengers adjusted themselves in the sleeping position. Some were in conversation with their neighbours. Others listened to the drugs man and yet others shouted him down to leave them in peace. He offered two of the wonder drug for the price of one and asked who would want to be the beneficiaries of the only ten bottles he had on the bus. Hands shut up and he started selling.

By this time the bus was negotiating its way up the steep hill that featured protective eucalyptus trees on the leeward side. When it stopped at the customs checkpoint that marked the end of town and the beginning of the long journey out of town, it stopped for the routine check on goods on board. At that point, the drug man left the bus.

When the bus started off again, the driver switched off the lights and turned on the music. It was bottle dance, the latest craze in the country. He changed cassettes one after the other. Now he was playing Ni Ken's "Taxi Driver" Some passengers fell asleep. These included Isidore Wamuvud who had not said a word to anybody since he waved goodbye to his son. But he did not feel lonely. He was thinking about the dossier in Ongola. He was also overwhelmed by the urge - inexplicable to him - to pray. He prayed and even when he fell asleep he continued to pray in his dreams. Thus began for him and the other 28 or so passengers, the six-hour night journey from Zamanda to Ongola, the capital.

When the vehicle was about an hour and a half from the town of Meyuf where such night buses pause for an hour's break, thus giving passengers time to have a bite, ease themselves and possibly stretch their legs, land then took off. Some passengers expressed impatience with the music. Some of them felt it was too loud while others complained it was repetitive and monotonous. This resulted in a quarrel with the driver who said he would neither change the music nor lower it. When asked why, he became even more irritated and much to the astonishment of passengers, warned that if he were harassed any more, he would crash the vehicle so that everybody would die. The men shouted insults at him and the women let out loud wails of exasperation. It was like some film.

An elderly passenger got up: "My son, are you saying death means nothing to you?"

"Nothing at all! Nothing! I don't care! And by the way, I'm not your son!" he snapped.

The elder turned to the passengers: "Ladies and gentlemen, you heard for yourselves what the young man said. My advice is that we leave him alone, whether the music is loud and boring or not. I think that when it comes to choosing between our lives and insistence on rights, we should choose our lives."

He sat down and all the agitated passengers said nothing more. Isidore Wamuvud for his part had taken out the family photographs and was looking at them one after the other. Although the monotony of the music also got on his nerves, he was perfectly comfortable with looking at the pictures over and over. He really did not know why he had brought the photographs with him. Even his wife had remarked that this was the first time he was asking for odd things like photographs to be put in his luggage. But at this moment, he was not thinking of the wedding suit that was also in his suitcase. A light sleep took control of him. Within seconds, he was back home, going to church with the family.

As they entered the Parish Church where they usually attended mass, his son Peter said to him: "Papa, look at the altar! I can see Jesus and Mary standing on either side of the priest!"

Further ahead at the front, the man who was sitting next to the driver was fighting a battle with sleep. He had just dreamed that the bus crashed and a number of people died, including himself and the driver. He had become so scared that he did not want to fall asleep again just in case that horrible dream came true. Although the dream involved the driver he did not have the courage to tell him so for two reasons. Firstly, recounting it would reawaken in him (the passenger) that forbid fear that he was eager to banish at all cost. Secondly, the driver was certainly not the kind of person who encouraged conversation. Since the quarrel he had with passengers about the music on board, he had not spoken to anyone.

Instead, his neighbour, a primary school teacher who had done some psychology noticed that in addition to his quarrelsome nature, the driver slammed the music to a stop. There was silence, apart from the snoring of those who were already far gone in sleep. So the driver was left to his own devices. His only company was the steering wheel. So he clung to it as if in search of some psychological fulfilment.

The road from Zamanda to Ongola was one of the major highways of the country. It was tarred, but like with most poorly thought out projects in the countries South of the Sahara, the road- signalling system left a lot to be desired. At bends, there were hardly any luminescent devices to guide drivers. The white were potholes here and there. But perhaps the greatest threat to security was the breakneck speed at which drivers drove. Even the big timber carriers and other vehicles of the sort that were expected to pull to the right and drive slowly behaved similarly. Drivers were always in a mad rush to overtake the one in front of them that made anyone wonder whether they were really going to a destination beyond the country. To make matters worse, the police and gendarmes who were supposed to ensure security on the roads were only interested in one thing: extorting money from commercial drivers, and where possible, private drivers too. They did so by systematically stopping an approaching driver, collecting his car papers and instructing him to park further ahead, out of view of curious passengers. The driver would then park and walk back to the officer where the deal took place. The security officials hardly ever inspected the state of the vehicles. As a result, many drivers drove around in what could be best described as death traps, unquestioned, unchallenged. Such was the state of the road on this day Isidore Wamuvud left for Ongola.

The night bus from Zamanda continued on its journey. The driver, still left to himself, readjusted his seat, having maintained one posture for too long. There was a timber lorry in front, moving too slowly for his liking. He attempted to overtake the lorry but quickly moved back into his lane when he realised there was an oncoming vehicle. Noticing that there was a bend ahead, he stayed behind the lorry waiting for the coast to be clear. By now he was feeling slightly sleepy. When he felt his pockets for a packet of cigarettes, he fond he had none. He was reluctant to ask passenger if anyone had a cigarette because of the way he had treated them. In any case, it looked like they were asleep. He wound down his window glass. Just then he found that it was safe for him to move out and overtake. Then he spotted an oncoming vehicle. After having hesitated, he decided the other vehicle was too far off. So he moved out. All of a sudden, there was a loud bang, and then a second one. His vehicle and the other one had run into each other and the one tailing him had run into the back of his own. The lorry driver who had been driving in front nearly lost control of his own vehicle but quickly brought it to a halt He got out of the vehicle.

What he saw made him weep loudly. "Please, come out and let's help! There is trouble here, oh!" he said to the two passengers travelling with him on the lorry.

The truck driver's passengers quickly set up long lines of grass on either side of the road to warn oncoming drivers that there was danger ahead. Vehicles that arrived at the scene stopped and their passengers descended. There was blood, human remains such as flesh, fingers, and hair, brain strewn all over the place. Lifeless bodies could be found in the two vehicles, some slightly injured and others seriously. A few passengers were still calling out for help. The driver of the bus from Zamanda and the teacher who sat by him and dreamed there was a crash, were among those who died on the spot.

At the time the crash happened, Isidore was asleep. Within seconds of the crash, he found himself out of his body, floating. In fact, the loud bang had served as a parting shot that suddenly forced him out of his body. As he floated over the scene of the accident, he saw the mangled remains of his bus, the other bus with which they clashed and the parked timber lorry. He saw people running about frantically pulling bodies here and there. In his own bus, he saw bodies lying on other bodies, some lifeless. Then he saw his own body, lying on top of the woman who had sat next to him. He saw helpers remove the bodies from the vehicles. He saw himself, or rather, his body being heaped into a vehicle, among other corpses.

"Am I dead?" he wondered? Then how is it I can see myself from where I am?"

He tried to look around him but only saw huge empty expanses of the sky. Or was it heaven? He tried to pinch himself to ensure he was not dreaming, but found he had no hands. He looked down on himself and found that where he was, he did not have a body. He was not even a body. He tried to talk, to call out to the people below at the scene of the accident, but no one appeared to be hearing him.

The next second, and I mean a second, he was floating over his home in Zamanda. It was about 1.30 am our own time. From up where he was, he could see all the rooms in the house and everything that was in it. The roof and walls were unusually transparent, like see-through glass. He saw his bedroom and his wife, fast asleep. He decided to enter the children's room and was there the next second. They were all asleep. He stood there, or rather, was suspended in the air for some seconds, contemplating the children. Then suddenly, without really knowing why, he thought:

"Oh my son, Peter, you are my rock. I know you will look after your mother and the other children very well."

"Papa!" grumbled Peter in his sleep as if he knew his father was there and had spoken to him.

At that point Isodore heard a distant voice: "Isidore, we are waiting for you!"

Suddenly, he was back at the scene of the accident where he saw everybody below but nobody below seemed to notice him above.

By now, nearly all the accident victims had been picked up, the lifeless ones loaded on the timber lorry and other vehicles that had arrived, and the injured ones ferried to the nearest hospitals. Helpers were still piecing together passengers' belongings. From up there, Isidore saw a gendarme opening his travelling suitcase. The latter took out the wedding suit his wife had packed, opened his copy of retirement file, looked at some photographs that were in the suitcase and closed it. Just then, someone else walked up to the gendarme.

"Don't close it yet officer. These other photographs might be his."

Another gendarme was looking through Isidore's wallet. In it, he found one photograph: that of a boy. And he thought to himself:

"This must be the next-of- kin."

Unknown to him, it was, indeed, it was Peter.

Up there where Isidore was, he saw and heard everything below. Yet he could not intervene.

Those were two different worlds.

"Isidore!" came a sharp call that made him start up. When he turned round he saw several women and men floating towards him. He recognised them as some of the fellow passengers of the bus they had travelled in.

"Come this way, all of you!" said a distant voice, to which they immediately turned.

Isidore saw something like a huge door open up in the sky and a huge spectrum-like bright beam out of it. A man in

123

immaculate white flowing gowns that like nothing Isidore had ever seen on earth led them into what one might describe as the most exquisite kingdom ever. There were marble-decorated sumptuous buildings, incredible gardens, roads and paths paved with gold and diamonds. it was a world beyond belief.

"Is this heaven?" Isidore wondered to himself.

"It is not heaven" responded the guide as if he had heard Isidore.

"Heaven is billions of times more attractive"

Then they arrived at a huge gate where another man opened a book, called out their names, one at a time and let them in. Isidore was the last to go in. But by the time it was his turn, he had started praying, saying: "Dear god, whatever it is that you decide about me, take me in as well. You can't bring me all this way to all of this and turn me back."

The new place they entered was even more beautiful than the previous one. The guide who did not introduce himself said the first place was called Achum, and the second, Azob. The more you are upgraded, the higher you go, and that all depended on the life you led on earth, he said. God made his commandments to help people live the right way. The next stage, he said was called Ikang. Isidore asked about how many of these stages were there there.

"Millions," said the guide. "The final one is God himself, the almighty, the summit, the apex, the culmination, the zenith, the end, and the omega, the levelling off. So far, only Jesus has got to that point. Only Jesus and perhaps Mary his mother."

"Perhaps? Why do you say, perhaps?" enquired Isidore, encouraged by the simplicity and modesty of the guide."

They kept walking, or perhaps, floating.

"Well, you can't be told everything now, can you? You have only just arrived...," he paused, and continued: "What you have to know now is that everything people do on earth is carefully noted down in the book of records up here. When you die as you people have just done, the book is consulted and you are sent to your own level, depending on your own deeds on earth. You must be made to visit each of the levels below in order to have an idea of what it is like, there. When you finally get to your own level, you stay there."

"And what happens after."

"Well, it depends on the creator. He may decide to promote you or demote you to a lower level. If he wishes, he can send you back to earth to give you another chance. But this may mean being born in another country and to totally different parents."

At that point, the guide led them to another gate. When it was opened, the light that came though was more beautiful than the previous one. The infrastructure was unbelievable.

"This must be Ikang," Isidore thought.

"You are right!" said the guide"

"Come this way, all of you!" said an old man with gray hair and gray beard sitting in the middle of six other people (three to his right and three to his left) at a great table.

"Line up here in the middle of the hall and come up to me one at a time!" he commanded.

The first person went up to the table, and running his finger through the book, the old man was saying:

"Isaac Akum... Isaac Akum... Yes! Here's his name. Satellite Number 3."

Just then, one of the several doors leading away from the great hall opened and Isaac Akum was led away through it.

As the door opened, Isidore caught a glimpse of what was beyond it and everything looked so beautiful that he thought he was dreaming. Again, the other passengers were all sent off through different so-called satellite doors.

When it came to his turn, he held his breath, not knowing to which door he would be sent, and whether his would be as beautiful as the others he had seen.

"Isidore Wamuvud! Satellite Number 7." He stepped forward and was promptly led away, much to his surprise, number 7 was much more attractive than all the others. What a heavenly kingdom it was!

Then, he heard his late father's voice call out to him. It was he. As he went towards his father, he saw his late mother, his late grand parents, uncles, aunts and friends. All of them looked very happy with themselves. Their presence did not look odd to Isidore who attempted to grab his father and hug him. But he found that although he was seeing his father he could not touch him, just as he had been unable to touch himself when he floated over the scene of the accident.

"Don't worry about it, son. Here in this world, we don't have bodies. We don't need them. We just exist. Come, I will show you round. As you will see, it's so great here. We enjoy ourselves very much. We like it here so much. We are told that since we are making progress, we'll soon be moved to the fourth plane, Ifoe, which is a lot better than this. Yet this one is already so good to be true that I wonder what the next will be like."

"But father, did you ever think of us while here?"

"Of course, we did and still do. Our prayer was that you people should join us here as soon as possible. And I am happy you are already here. You see, life on earth is suffering and nothing more than suffering. T he real life to be enjoyed is here, not there. That is why one of the first reactions of a new born baby, that is, a human being entering the world for the first time, is to utter a cry. He is moaning his entry into the world of suffering. On the other hand, usually when people are dying, that is when they have caught a glimpse of this our own new world, they wish very quickly to join it, so what we call birth and life on earth are really death, and what we call death is actually birth into the new world, the new kingdom. Come; let me show you the inner chamber!

****

The first time news of the accident went public as such was the following morning, on the 6.30 morning news in English at the national radio station. The Gendarmerie brigade that had jurisdiction over Ekang the accident village, Ngoloma, had called the radio station and broken the news. But it was patchy in the sense that names of victims had not been communicated.

The national station had then contacted the provincial station, in Loumd, near Ekang, which had sent the missing details through on the 7 o'clock news from the accident spot.

Mr. Atia, Isidore Wamuvud's neighbour at whose place he took his telephone calls, heard the 6 o'clock news item but for some strange reason, the thought did not cross his mind that Isidore could be involved. So, he decided to continue listening to the radio. Television was out of the question because the country only had one channel that opened at midday. Private television stations were still in their infancy and so could not be relied on. When the 7 o'clock news came, confirmation came like a sledgehammer. Mr. Atia leapt out of his seat and called out his wife. But she was out.

He hurried to Isidore's house. When he got nearer, he found her by the kitchen, readjusting the dress of one of the girls, as she got ready for school.

When they greeted each other, Mr. Atia did not have the courage to broach the topic, the more so as it looked as though Mrs. Wamuvud was unaware of the accident. He said good-bye to her and just as he was making about turn, she said.

"But Mr. Atia where were you going?"

"I was just coming here to see if everything was alright."

"Yes, we're fine, I am okay and the children are okay... at least as far as I know."

The reason she was cautious, although she did not tell him, was that on that very night, that is, the night her husband left for Ongola, he appeared in her dream and said: "Lydia, look after the children. Peter will assist you. He takes my place," then he disappeared. She got up and could not understand or believe what had happened.

What did he mean? Was he going to die? Was there going to be an accident? Anyway, she went back to bed.

At about 8 o'clock, Mr. Atia heard wailing from his neighbour's quarters. He and his wife to whom he had broken the news but asked her not to say anything to anyone, hurried to Wamuvud's compound. There a huge crowd had gathered and more people were joining them. Wamuvud's children were weeping and being consoled by family members.

Mrs. Wamuvud was simply throwing herself against the ground and saying: "Yes! I knew it! He told me in a dream last night! He said he was going to the capital to chase his retirement benefit dossier...now, where is the money? And where is he? He has left me in the middle of nowhere with seven children... why? Why me God? ... What have I done to deserve this?"

In the evening when things were calmer and some of Isodore's relatives had arrived, they held a meeting during which two brothers were dispatched to the Ndangoua divisional hospital to collect Isidore's body. It would take three days, considering the distance and administrative bottlenecks involved in getting a corpse out of the mortuary. In that country, bureaucracy was grossly exaggerated.

In the mean time, the family would be making the necessary arrangements for burial. The priest had to be contacted about a requiem mass, radio announcements made to inform people, the compound spruced up for the reception of guests. Above all, perhaps, money had to be raised for entertainment. Mrs. Wamuvud was lucky in that her husband's brothers and even friends agreed to chip in.

When Wamuvud's corpse reached his compound, his wife's feelings were so high that she refused to see it. She wept bitterly, again throwing herself down several times.

All that while friends and relatives, notably her sisters consoled her, reminding her that even if her husband had gone, she still had the children, and that was something; it wasn't nothing. Slowly but steadily, she regained control of herself. When the coffin was opened, she found that her husband was dressed in the wedding suit he had insisted on taking along.

"So that's why he asked for this suit!" she burst out again, sobbing. "So that's why he wanted it? For the first time in the twenty years of our marriage, he asked me to include his wedding suit among his travel items. Now look at what has happened!"

Her sisters held her, also weeping, and sat her down. It was about 3 o'clock in the afternoon. It was Friday, exactly one week since she and her husband discussed the Ongola trip in bed. Later at five o'clock, the requiem mass would take place at the nearby St. Martin de Porres Catholic Church. That night there would be wake keeping. The following day, Saturday, at eleven o'clock, there would be burial, at the church. The Parish Priest. Father Leo Amabo had already given his accord.

During the requiem mass, Father Amabo bitterly called on the government to bring a halt to the costly torture civil servants went through by going to the national capital to chase dossiers which ought to progress normally and automatically. Why were the authorities letting this happen? Why could they not decentralise services so that dossiers were treated at the provincial, or even divisional level? If Isidore Wamuvud had not undertaken the perilous journey, he might not have died, at least, not when it happened.

But then again, that might not be the entire story, for God in his all knowing, all powerful ways could indeed draw straight lines in a crooked way, maybe it was his wish for Isidore to come 'home' now. It should not be forgotten that man proposes but God disposes.

Whatever anybody thought or said, Isidore was dead and gone and nobody could do anything about it. All that could be done now was praying to God for the repose of his soul.

The all-night wake keeping was animated by the popular Benson, a local musician who quickly established himself in the town and beyond, as an unequal able wake keeping animator, using his all purpose piano and stereo set. On that Friday night, he was at his best.

Moved by his music and the lyrics, a lot of people danced in the impromptu circle in the yard. In the middle of the table, was the coffin half open for people to see the man laying in state, as they filed past.

As usual, Benson played improvised lyrics, many of them well known to the dancing and chanting teeming population. He sang about Isidore's birth and upbringing, his education, his work history, his family and the fact that the government had killed him as it had killed many others before him by obliging them to spend a lot of money and time chasing files in the capital.

Wamuvud's wife, clad in white and a white veil, sat a few metres from the coffin, flanked by relatives comforting her. A few steps away, one of her husband's brothers gave instructions. She could not hear what he was saying, but she noticed the man was pointing to Peter's father's traditional cap. She also noticed that the said man was the successor to her late husband's father, thus the uncle of Peter's who would eventually install him as her husband's successor. Just then some people, who had filed past the corpse, came over to her to present their condolences and she lost track of Peter and his uncle.

The burial that took place the following day was well attended, which in a way was a successful testimony of Isidore Wamuvud's popularity. Peter ate and drank, which was good because, otherwise, there have been a lot of criticisms with remarks such as:

"What kind of funeral is this at which one has been offered neither food nor drink? Not even a beer, and not even a glass of palm wine?

Mrs. Wamuvud adjusted bit by bit to the loss of her husband. With her efforts that consisted of selling food in a small makeshift restaurant and the help of her husband's relatives, she kept the family going.

Often, she thought about her husband's unpaid benefits lying somewhere in Ongola, that is, if the money had not been embezzled, knowing the way things were done in the country.

One afternoon, Mrs. Wamuvud was surprised by a visit from the provincial delegate of culture, her husband's boss before he went on retirement.

This was a year after her husband died. The visitor came to find out about her husband's benefits. In the end, they both decided that since he was travelling to the capital the following week, she should put up a letter for the attention of the Minister of Finance, stating her plight since her husband died. That, she did.

Three months later, she was surprised to receive a reply signed by the Minister himself. In it, he named some documents she had to prepare. After that, she was to travel to Ongola and see him. That was very odd because in that country, Kamanga, it was rare for Ministers to respond to private correspondences, although they had the means and the manpower.

When she got to Ongola and went to the Minister's cabinet, she was made to fill out the booking form. She could not believe it when the footman came in and said:

"Madame Wamuvud, le ministre vous recevra maintenant".

As soon as the Minister saw her enter, he got up, shook her hand and said in halting English:

"Welcome Madam! Sorry about what happened to your husband. So you have not been paid any money yet"

"No, your Excellency"

"Okay" he said, getting up and walking to the window. He pulled aside the curtain and looked down from his fifth floor office. He could see reduced figures of people walking on the road leading to the old presidential palace. There were children among them, some walking, others being carried.

Turning round abruptly, he said to Mrs. Wamuvud;

"You have any children?"

"Yes, your Excellency"

"How many"

131

"Seven"

"That's a lot". By this time he was back at his table. He picked up the telephone and sent for the Director of General Administration.

"Did you bring the documents I asked for?"

"Yes your Excellency" "Good, the Director of General administration will handle your problem in person. Everything will be okay."

"Thank you, your Excellency."

When the Director came in, the Minister said to him in French

"Mrs. Wamuvud is all the way from Zamanda, she lost her husband, a retired civil servant last year. He was chasing his retirement benefits when he died. Collect Mrs. Wamuvud's documents and make sure all her husband's entitlements are paid.

"A vos ordres, Excellence!" said the Director as he collected the file from Mrs. Wamuvud.

The Director left promptly and as soon as he got to his office, he started making telephone calls to the people involved in the treatment of the dossier.

"Thank you very much, your Excellency!"

"Oh no, that's okay. That's why I am here. That's what the prime Minister and the President want us to do. Here is my card, if you have any problems, do not hesitate to call me.

As he headed for the door, the Minister called her back.

"Take this, for transport money back to Zamanda, and greet your children for me".

It was fifty thousand francs! Too good to be true, for before travelling to Ongola Mrs. Wamuvud could barely find the sum of thirty thousand francs. The fateful day her husband travelled to the capital, he only had twenty thousand francs.

Four months later, Mrs. Wamuvud was called to the Ministry and paid a first instalment of one million francs, which represented about half of the total amount due. She

132

was given a document stating that the rest would be paid in six month's time. Her joy was total.

Shortly afterwards, the Minister of Finance addressed a proposal to prime Minister, on the decentralisation of payments for not only retirement benefits but also several other types of entitlements.

If the prime Minister gave his approval, there would be less travel to the capital by civil servants in the provinces and more action in each province in the provincial capital. Exactly nine months later, the bill was passed in the national Assembly; five days after, the President of the republic promulgated it.

8

The turned tides

As soon as the metal gate swung open with a clatter the tore the silence of the night, Ndi sat up in bed mechanically. He had only been half asleep, as usual. He tapped his senior brother, Victor, on the shoulder:

Ni Victor! Ni Victor! It's Papa."

Victor, who had been fast asleep, quickly sat up and started rubbing his eyes with his right hand. He was still feeling sleepy. That was hardly surprising because Victor was the sleepy man of the house. At school his mates teased him by saying he had sleeping sickness. Of all the four children, all of whom were boys with Victor being the first, he was the one who could fall asleep anywhere, anytime. You could be lying on the same bed with Victor and conversing with him only to find that although he was the one who just spoke, he was already snoring.

Their father's violent knocks at the door and yelling suddenly got both Victor and Ndi on their feet. Fright grabbed them as they stood there by the window, seeing their father through the window blind but being too frightened to go and open the door, for, when he was in such a mood, it meant he was drunk - which was often - he beat up their mother and sometimes, when he felt like it, he beat them too. He seemed to enjoy doing this, which was what the boys could not understand.

"Is there no one in this house to open this bloody door before I break it down?" he barked as he banged at the door.

"I am here! I am coming!" his wife said as she merged from the kitchen and went to the door, wiping her wet hands on her dress.

"Well, then, why don't you bloody open this bloody door, you bastard?"

She said nothing but opened the door respectfully. As soon as the door opened, she was greeted by a strong smell of alcohol reaching her from her husband, as they stood there momentarily face-to-face. Although the smell was offensive, she could not reveal her revulsion, for fear of her husband pouncing on her. She knew he often did so when drunk. Sometimes when he was even sober, he would still thrash her. He told her once he was hitting her that he was doing so because she had removed his hat from one kitchen stool and put it on another.

"Don't let me beat you!"

What have I done, now?"

"What have you done? Must you do something before I beat you? I can beat you when you have done nothing, just as I can beat you when you have done something. I can beat you for sport, to exercise my arm. Ha! Ha! Ha!"

****

As soon as James Wirngo entered the house - the sitting room to be more precise - he flung his dripping umbrella on the sofa, trying to look more angry than he was, just to find an excuse to beat his wife, yet again.

"The umbrella is wet!" said his wife as she attempted to remove it.

"Leave it there or I'll kick your..."

"But it's wet. It will soak the seat."

"I say, leave it there, you bitch," he yelled at her, as he rushed towards her and rained blows on her. She fell and started weeping.

Just then, Victor and Ndi who had heard the noise, and above all their mother crying, opened the door that led to the sitting room from the bedrooms.

"Go back to bed, you dirty rats!" barked their father.

Promptly they closed the door and returned to their room. But they, too, like their mother, were in tears, although unlike her, they did so in low tones, for fear of their father.

135

James stood over his wife as she spread herself on the floor of the sitting room, sobbing and wreathing in pain. "You are a good for nothing. You hear me? A good for nothing!" he snapped at her.

Thereupon, he trudged to the bedroom, slamming the door behind him.

Within minutes he was already snoring. No wonder his wife, Pauline, was fond of teasing Victor by remarking that he and his father were the same when it came to sleep. Within her, she prayed that he would not grow into his father's violent habits.

When Pauline herself got into the bedroom, she found all of her husband in bed - shirt, tie, trousers, coat, socks and shoes. Despite this gross act, she did not take offence. Devotedly, she undressed him and dressed him up in his pyjamas. Despite all the movements his wife subjected him to while changing him, James Wirngo slept as profoundly as a baby.

"My God! How Victor takes so much after him!" she thought.

Pauline was, however not surprised, at her husband sleeping with his clothes on, for he had done so several times before. Once when he returned from work at about 4.30 pm and after complaining that he was tired, he went straight to bed as he was dressed, even taking with him his briefcase and umbrella. By the time she got to the bedroom, and that was only five minutes later, he was fast asleep. It was she who took away the umbrella and briefcase and changed him.

The children felt a lot of sympathy for their mother whom they saw as a powerless, defenceless, innocent victim. Sometimes when their father was beating her, they (but especially the two eldest) would clench their fists, gnash their teeth and curse him. Unfortunately for them there was nothing they could do but curse in hiding because they feared he might also unleash his wrath on them. And that was something they shuddered to think about. Surely, he did not thrash them as much as he thrashed their mother, but still, they were never out of the woods.

One evening when their father returned from one of his drinking sprees and sat down for his meal, he did something that almost claimed the life of Asongwed, the youngest of the four boys in the house. What happened was that when their father sat at table and started eating, he ordered the four-year old Asongwed to bring his slippers from the bedroom. The boy left promptly but returned with his father's sandals that he confidently placed at his feet.

"What have you brought me, you little devil!" said Wirngo, as he stood violently and kicked the boy in the buttocks. The kick was so strong that it raised the boy and made him land face down on the concrete floor.

When his mother heard him shouting, she rushed to the scene from the kitchen weeping. But she knew if she said anything her husband would grow wilder.

"Leave him where he is, woman!" He barked.

"But he is crying. So, he must have fallen. He has bruises all over his face!" she said as she herself started shouting for help.

"I say leave him! Leave him! It will teach him to obey simple instructions. "

"Instructions? What has he failed to do..."

"Mamma! Mamma!" cried little Asongwed, clinging to his mother's wrappa.

"Yes, my child. Mamma is here."

Just then Victor and Mumbe came in through the front door. Before any of them could say anything their father ordered them to leave. So, they went out. They were particularly disturbed because although their little brother had bruises and was bleeding, it did not seem to bother their father.

Turning to their mother, he snapped.

"Take that bastard and get out of here both of you."

Then he sat back at table and continued his meal as if nothing had happened.

"Come and clear off these dishes," he said to Victor.

It was 7.00 pm on that day. So without telling anyone where he was going - as that was not unusual - he picked up his hat and umbrella and left the house. No one was bold enough to ask him where he was going, let alone when he was returning.

****

When Wirngo returned home, it was late - 3.25pm. He was drunk. His clothes were soiled, which meant he had fallen several times as he struggled home. He stank of alcohol. Despite his state, he still entered his compound in a defiant mood:

"Where is that ... that ...bitch of a woman?... I will teach... teach ... teach her a lesson..."

He knocked at the door twice, but since it was locked from inside and there was no one by it, he kept knocking. Then suddenly, he hurled himself at it. Having been enfeebled by drink, he was the one who was sent crashing down. Somehow, he mustered enough energy to stand up. As he reached out for the doorknob, the door suddenly flung open and since he was half leaning on it, he went crashing inwards. His wife's attempt to catch him failed. He was a tall man with a heavy built while his wife was lean and short. As he fell she screamed:

"Oh! Oh! Please, don't."

She reached out, grabbed him by both hands and helped him to his feet. When he got up all dirty, one would have thought he would thank the poor woman. But he did not.

"You bitch! Why did you make me fall?"

"I? I made you fall? How?"

"Shut up, you bastard! ..." he said as he slapped her. At once Pauline started crying. As she walked away from him, he caught her by her wrappa and pulled so hard that the wrappa came off her body, thus exposing her underwear.

"Oh my God! What are you doing to me, Ni?" she said, both embittered and embarrassed.

"What am I doing? I... I... am exposing you. Can't you see? You are useless! Useless!" he said, staggering into a chair. The next minute he was fast asleep, snoring. She had gone to the bedroom to put on something. By the time she came back, her eyes were still wet.

Seeing her husband in such a state and being the dutiful wife she was, she led him half asleep to the bedroom, undressed him helped him to bathe, dressed him up and put him to bed. All he could say with the distance and nonchalance typical of drunkards was:

"Pauline, where am I?"

****

Reading this one would think Wirngo was always like that. But far from it. The early part of their marriage was a happy one.

He had started off as a civil servant. He was head of the small claims bureau in the Ministry of Natural Resources. He had entered the civil service after earning three subjects at the London R.S.A. examination in Law, Economics and Accountancy. After working in the Ministry for eleven years, he learned that as part of government structural readjustment of the economy, the civil service was being streamlined with some civil servants being retrenched. However, he was told that government would pay a substantial lump sum to those willing to go on early retirement. He accepted it and was paid three million francs in addition to his pension. However, it was a disaster because he soon squandered the money. He rejected all the useful advice his wife gave him.

"Oh! Stop your foolish talk, woman. This is money I earned; nothing bad about it. It's not money I stole."

"Yes, but the problem is that the rate at which you are spending it, very soon there will be nothing left."

"And so what? By the way, shut up! Who do you think you are talking to? Are you trying to teach me?"

"No, there are no lessons I have to give you. I just thought..."

"Enough, woman! Or else I'll give you the beating of your life."

Pauline said no more.

Today, James was destitute, or nearly so. The pension he received was really not enough to cater for the basic needs of the family. As a result his wife started doing some petty trading - selling foodstuffs and ingredients in a makeshift provision store near the house. Her customers were mainly neighbours or the odd passerby. With what she earned, she was barely able to keep the home going. For his part he called himself a businessman, although to be frank, no one knew exactly what he was doing. Nonetheless, things did not always work out that way, because often, when he ran out of money, he would pressurise Pauline to give him some. Normally, she would not mind bailing him out. However, problems soon arose between them when he went as far as demanding money she had set aside for essential needs such as a child falling ill, food getting finished, and so on.

One day he felt like going out for a drink.

"Pauline, dear. Can I have some money, please?"

"How much money, Ni?"

"Three thousand francs."

"I can't give you that amount."

"Then how much can you give?"

"I don't know."

"How much do you have?"

"Five thousand francs."

"Then it's easy. Give me three thousand francs and keep the other two thousand."

"No. This money is for emergencies."

"And you do not think I have an emergency now?"

"No, I don't think. It's for emergencies such a child falling ill, or something."

"Why should a child fall ill only when I have taken money from you?"

"It's not that. It's that..."

"It's that all. Give me the money before I get angry with you."

"No, I can't."

Suddenly, he changed his tone and ordered her to give him the money or be beaten up."

"I can't. I've told you what the money is for."

At that point, Pauline had to go and water the flowers. Her husband followed her there with the intention of sweet-talking her. If it did not work, he would then use force, as usual.

"What is this you are doing to me, Pauline? You want me to go down on my knees before you give me a little money for a drink?"

"No, my dear. It's not that. It's just that you are refusing to understand."

"Understand what! What is there to understand when you haven't given me what I am asking for?"

"What I mean is..." she paused to throw a bowl of water on the flowers.

"Can't you stop what you are doing to listen to me for one minute!" he snapped, pulling her by the right hand and slapping her in the face. Then he landed her another slap on the cheek and then gave her a kick on the buttocks. Thereupon she fell on one of the flowerbeds bruising her face against the wall.

She was screaming. This was one of the few moments when he beat her during the day. Usually, it was at night after he had returned from his drinking.

Hearing their mother scream, the children - all of them - came out and when they saw what was going on, they started crying, too. Neighbours came out, too although this was nothing new to them.

John Buteh, the veterinary man who was one of the nearest neighbours walked straight to Mr. Wirngo and spoke to him harshly.

"Neighbour, what is the matter here again? This is ridiculous. Why this unending war with your wife? Is she a beast or a human being?"

"Yes, Mr. John, ask him what I have done for him to beat me today. Simply because he asked me for money which I did not have, he..."

"Shut up, woman before I give you more of it! And you this... you call yourself what? A Vet? I call you a 'wet' because you are wet, all wet. And you dare come to my house and ask me questions about my private life?"

"But that's not fair, Mr. Wirngo. It's not today that you and I have known each other. We grew up together as kids and..."

"Don't tell lies. We didn't grow up together. I don't even know you, you impostor."

"Listen to me, Wirngo." said Mr. John, his temper rising. "The problem is not me but your wife, this poor woman whom you batter everyday. if you did not have a boy child you would have insulted God for not giving you a successor. But he has given you up to four boys. So what more do you want?" Yet you call yourself a Christian..."

"Shut up, you bastard," said Wirngo, charging at Buteh. "Don't preach to me! Who are you to preach to me? I treat my wife as I like. It's my business, not yours."

"But, Wirngo, what do you want? You got married to Pauline when she was successfully running a computerised secretariat. You pulled her away from her job and made her a full time housewife."

"Oh! Come on! Don't talk about things you do not know. She works. I opened a business for her."

"Oh, work? You call what she does work? She sells petty kitchen ingredients and other materials on a side street stall. That's all. It's not even what one can call a provision store. Look at how you are wasting a whole HND holder in Secretarial Studies and Office Management. She was commanding a whole secretariat before. If you want me to tell you, Wirngo, I will. You have wasted this woman's life."

"Wasted her life, you say? I have given her children, you bastard."

"Children? What children? The same ones you terrorise when you humiliate their mother before their very eyes?"

"Buteh is right." chipped in Boniface the carpenter who did most of the carpentry jobs in the New Layout quarter where they lived. "Look at the poor woman," Boniface said not necessarily addressing himself to anyone in particular. "She is weeping now as she wept yesterday and will weep tomorrow. Look here, Buteh, "he said turning to his neighbour, 'you asked me to make another bed for your children. That was last year. When you collected the bed you promised to pay me at the end of the month. Eight months passed without you giving me a single franc. In the end it was your wife who paid for the bed. There are many other examples I could cite here now, but i am sure you wouldn't want me to do so."

"Why not? Go on and name them, Wirngo shouted, charging at Buteh. By this time, Pauline was up and being comforted by some women neighbours. A large crowd of neighbours and also passersby had also gathered at the scene of what had now degenerated into a generalised quarrel. People who heard the quarrelling voices joined the crowd to find out what was going on.

"Na weti dey happen here?" asked a plantain seller as he pulled up with his bike laden with plantain bunches.

"I no know. Me, too, I dey just come like this," replied the unknown man he had gone up to.

"Na weti dey for here, Madam?" the plantain man asked as he nudged the woman next to him.

"No be na Wirngo again?"

"Wirngo na who, Madam?"

"How? You no know Wirngo? Some man dey for this quarter wey he no know Wirngo? No be dat mimbo man wey he dey so so beat ye woman?"

"Na di woman dat, Madam?" the plantain seller asked, as he pointed to Pauline, obviously the only weeping woman on the crowd.

Meanwhile Wirngo had flung himself at Buteh and both of them started their own fight. But the men in the crowd quickly pounced at them and tore them apart.

Just then, Buteh's ten-year-old son, Madi, hurried to his father in the crowd, whispered something in his ear and his father left with him for their house. It was not clear what son told father. But the result was that he immediately left the scene of the conflict. Had he given his father a message from himself or had his mother sent him to him.

Shortly afterwards the crowd started dispersing. Without saying a word to anyone, Wirngo left and returned to his house. His wife tarried behind in the company of the other women. By the time she got to the front door, her husband brushed past her without saying a word. He was carrying his umbrella and hat. It was late afternoon. She did not say anything to him. He did not talk to her either. Neither did he hit her, threaten her or even insult her. Deep within her heart, she had no doubt where her husband was going: to the village square to drink. And she was right because he returned home late - at about 3 o'clock in the morning, drunk and smelling of alcohol. But for once he was not loud or violent. He simply knocked a few times at the door and she opened it. He went in without talking to her or even answering her greetings. He went straight to the bedroom and flung himself in bed. His wife removed his clothes and shoes and socks and dressed him up in his pyjamas.

During the night, Pauline prayed to God Almighty that if this was the welcome change coming over her husband, then might God be praised. As she put it, she had suffered for too long in this marriage in which she had made all kinds of sacrifices to no avail. Had it not been for her children, she would have quit a long time. But she always wondered what would happen to them if she left. Would she be allowed to take them away? If not, how could she live without them.

Nonetheless, one of the reasons for deciding to sit through the struggle was her own father who said that whatever was the case, on no account should she abandon her matrimonial home.

"Look here, my daughter, marriage is like that. It's give and take. And if you should ask me, the worst type of woman is the one who has walked out of her marriage. You marry for better or for worse. Besides, if you quit, it will be a personal failure on my part, because, what education would people think I gave you."

But left to Pauline's mother, she should have left Wirngo and brought the children with her. Whenever mother and daughter were together and lamented at how badly Pauline's marriage had gone, they wept together. But Pauline's mother had a problem in that although she wanted her daughter to walk out on Wirngo, "in order to teach him a lesson," Pauline's father held the contrary view. And since he was the one who had the last word in the family, she capitulated.

Pauline's prayer worked for one day, two days, three and a week! She became so excited that she ran to her mother who was really her best friend and broke the news to her.

"Mama, it seems he has changed. He hasn't beaten me for a month!"

"God is great, my daughter! He has heard your prayer and answered it. Can't you see?"

Unfortunately for Pauline, that honeymoon was not going to last long because her husband relapsed and started beating her up again. The beatings became even more frequent than before. One night after one of those rows when Wirngo was already snoring in bed beside his wife, she took out her rosary and prayed thus:

"Heavenly Father, you know only too well what pain I have gone through in this marriage. I plead with you to forgive me for any wrongdoing to you, my husband or anyone else. I also now surrender myself and this cavalry to you. Only you alone will tell me what to do."

A couple of hours later when she was asleep, her mother's late grandfather appeared to her in a dream. He held her hand and they walked along a very beautiful road. Then they came to a junction where there were children playing in a garden and men playing cards on the open air benches in the garden. Everyone was so beautiful. He said to her, pointing to one of them.

"Pauline."

"Yes, Grandpa."

"Do you see that man in a white shirt about to place a card on the table."

"Yes, Grandpa, I see him."

As she spoke, she realised it was her class seven teacher in primary school, the teacher of hers, who throughout her seven years in primary school, beat her more than anyone else. AS she kept looking at home, she suddenly turned into her husband.

"Yes, Grandpa. That's my husband."

"You mean the man who torments you?"

"Yes, Grandpa. But what's he doing here? Where am I?"

"Don't worry about that, child. You are in my world. I was sent to tell you how to solve him like a Mathematics problem. Remember you were always good at Maths at school."

"Yes, Grandpa. But..."

"Ah! I didn't bring you here to ask questions. Listen. When next he beats you, stand up for yourself, stamp your feet angrily and shout: 'enough is enough, Wirngo! I've put up with you for too long.' Then charge at him and you will see what will happen."

"But, Grandpa, what..."

By now her grandfather had disappeared, the dream had come to an end and she was once in bed by her snoring husband.

****

The following night when James returned home late and drunk, trouble started again. But then she suddenly remembered the dream and thought that perhaps she ought to do as her grandfather bid her.

Just as she was thinking, she heard her husband banging at the door and yelling insults at her. As she hurried towards the door from the bedroom, she heard a loud bang. When she got nearer, she found that her husband had actually broken down the door and it had fallen inwards on the floor. Her heart missed a beat and she was really terrified. Her husband was furious and muttering to himself as he charged at her. At that point, many thoughts came to her head, one of which was that although her husband had created many scenes before, never had he gone as far as breaking down the door. She also observed that never before had he looked so furious.

As he staggered towards her, he lashed out blows that she dodged and said to her: "You bitch! You told people I am a weakling. I'll show you that I am strong."

"What? I told people? Which People?"

"Don't ask me what you already know, you idiot."

"But I didn't."

"Yes, you did, you bitch. You deny it, liar?"

"But..."

"Don't you 'but' me..."

All this while Pauline was dodging her husband's blows. Then as he gave chase, she moved round to the other side of the dinning table. As he continued the chase, they moved around the table.

The children hearing the noise came out of their rooms and watched from a safe distance. They clung to each other. Although none of them spoke, they were all filled with revulsion for their father and wished that something bad would really happen to him so that he would leave their mother alone.

At one point, Wirngo, realising that his wife was back-against-the-wall, suddenly pushed the table towards her so that she was caught between the table and the wall. Now that she was cornered, he lashed out at her and this time caught her thrice.

Suddenly, as if stung or even possessed, she grabbed the side of the table nearest to her and summoning the last iota of energy in her, she pushed the table back at him. So strong was her push that the table brought her husband crashing on the floor. Like a cat, Pauline leapt at him and started raining blows at him.

"I am fed up! I have had enough of you! What do you take me for? What..."

At that point, the children watching their parents from their safe corner exchanged glances of surprise and leapt for joy. They felt like joining their mother in punishing their father, but lacked the courage to do so.

Neighbours hearing the shouts and screams came rushing. They were surprised to find Pauline, for once, holding her husband down and beating him. Buteh and Boniface stepped forward and pulled Pauline from off her husband. Then they helped him to his feet. His wife looked triumphant. He looked worn out, bruised and humiliated. Even he could not understand how it happened.

"What happened?" asked one man as he came in.

"We don't know yet. But we found Pauline on top of her husband, beating him," said Boniface.

"You mean the tides have turned?" asked another.

"Yes, they have," said Boniface. "And who says a woman too couldn't lie on top of a man?"

From that day Pauline learned to stand up for herself. She disagreed with her husband when he was wrong. He, too, learned to respect her. And thus, the neighbourhood became living witnesses to the transformation of a human being for the better.